MARVEL

BLACK PANTHER
THE YOUNG PRINCE

MARVEL

BLACK PANTHER
THE YOUNG PRINCE

RONALD L. SMITH

LOS ANGELES • NEW YORK

© 2018 MARVEL
All rights reserved. Published by Marvel Press,
an imprint of Disney Book Group. No part of this book may be
reproduced or transmitted in any form or by any means, electronic or
mechanical, including photocopying, recording, or by any information
storage and retrieval system, without written permission from the
publisher. For information address Marvel Press,
125 West End Avenue, New York, New York 10023.

First Hardcover Edition, January 2018
First Paperback Edition, January 2019
10 9 8 7 6 5 4 3 2 1
FAC-020093-18327
Printed in the United States of America

This book is set in Adobe Caslon Pro, Century Gothic/Monotype;
Printhouse, Roughhouse/House Industries; The Hand/S&C Type,
KGGodGaveMeYou/Fontspring
Designed by Marci Senders

Library of Congress Control Number for Hardcover: 2017906486
ISBN 978-1-368-00849-5

Visit www.DisneyBooks.com
www.Marvel.com

SUSTAINABLE Certified Sourcing
FORESTRY
INITIATIVE www.sfiprogram.org
SFI-00993

THIS LABEL APPLIES TO TEXT STOCK

For Adriann Ranta Zurhellen
A Super-Hero Agent

MARVEL

BLACK PANTHER

THE YOUNG PRINCE

CHAPTER ONE

The young prince fled through the forest, his pursuer hot on his heels.

His heartbeat thundered in his ears. He couldn't give up. Not this time.

He ducked a low-hanging branch and splashed through a muddy creek. His attacker was gaining on him. He could almost hear his breath on his back.

There—

Up ahead, a fallen tree.

He jumped, and—

His legs were pulled out from under him.

He crashed to the ground. Strong hands grabbed his ankles. He tried to break free, but his foe rolled him over and pinned him to the damp forest floor.

"I got you this time," M'Baku hissed. "Nowhere to run now."

The young prince gasped for air. "Okay, okay," he said. "You won. *This time.* Wanna go again?"

M'Baku rose and extended a hand, pulling his friend up with a firm grip.

"If it hadn't been for that log . . ." the prince started, brushing dirt from his linen trousers.

M'Baku smirked. "Excuses, excuses. I beat you fair and square, T'Challa."

T'Challa looked up and cocked his head. "Don't you know it's not smart to mock your superiors?"

M'Baku bowed low in fake sincerity. "Oh, mighty prince, please forgive me for the error of my ways. I am but a lowly servant."

T'Challa rolled his eyes.

M'Baku was T'Challa's closest friend. They did everything together—sneaking out when they were supposed to be studying, playing practical jokes on unsuspecting victims, and sometimes venturing as far as the neighboring city, even though T'Challa was supposed to have a personal guard with him at all times. Like now, for instance.

One thing he would never forget was the look on his father's face when he came home late once after being gone for hours. *The whole tribe was out looking for you,* his father had said. *There are dangers in the forest, T'Challa. You must always be wary.*

It was a lesson he took to heart, but every now and then, M'Baku egged him on, daring him to break every rule the king laid out for him.

The forest around them was vast, teeming with lush vegetation and towering trees that seemed to brush the very heavens. In the distance, a mountain range rose high above the clouds, the midday sun glinting off its white peaks.

"C'mon," M'Baku said. "I'll race you to the river's edge."

T'Challa wiped sweat from his forehead with the back of his hand. He was tired, but he couldn't let M'Baku know that. He crouched low, ready to sprint.

"Go!" M'Baku shouted.

Both boys dashed through the forest, trampling broken branches and leaping over fallen tree stumps. This was when T'Challa felt most alive, in the woods with his best friend, finding adventure and escaping his royal duties. Out here, he wasn't a prince. He was just a kid.

M'Baku passed him, kicking up dirt in his path. T'Challa pushed himself as hard as he could. He was gaining on him.

But M'Baku had suddenly stopped on the path.

T'Challa swerved at the last minute, missing him by inches. He bent and rested his hands on his knees, winded. "Why'd you stop?"

M'Baku slowly raised his hand and pointed. "Look."

A few feet ahead of them, a man lay slumped against a tree. He wore a military uniform, but it was one T'Challa had never seen before.

"Is he dead?" M'Baku whispered.

T'Challa didn't answer, but took a few steps forward. The man had a bandage around his leg, where his pants had been ripped. Blood soaked it red. "Help," he croaked out. "Please. Help me."

T'Challa took another wary step. He didn't know who the man was, but his father always said it was his duty to help those in trouble.

A rustling in the bushes made them both pause.

M'Baku started. "What was that?"

T'Challa didn't have time to answer, as four figures stepped through the trees.

CHAPTER TWO

They were tall. And they were all women. Tribal markings adorned their faces. They were the Dora Milaje, the king's private bodyguards and the fiercest warriors in the country.

Hints of gold and silver glinted from the bracelets and cuffs around their necks and arms. Their spear points sparkled in the sun that filtered through the canopy of trees above them. T'Challa had seen those spears before, and knew that they also doubled as giant batons equipped with electrical charges.

T'Challa tensed.

"My prince," one of them said, stepping forward with

a slight bow and placing her right hand on her heart. "The king has demanded your presence."

T'Challa was taken aback. "This man," he started, coming back to the moment. "He needs help. He was mauled, or—"

"We will take care of him," the woman said, without the slightest hint of sympathy.

The man tried to get up, but one of the Dora Milaje thrust her spear just inches from his neck. "Don't leave me with them," he pleaded, his eyes going wide. "Please!"

T'Challa didn't want to leave, but he had to obey his father's command—even if he did feel sorry for this strange man and whatever plight he had fallen into. He turned to M'Baku. "I'll see you later. I have to—"

"He is also summoned," the woman interrupted him. "Both of you." She cast a sidelong glance at M'Baku. *Now.*

The young prince hesitated with each step he took.

"What does he want with me?" M'Baku whispered, a hint of fear in his voice.

"I don't know," T'Challa replied. He was busy thinking of what could have happened to the injured man. He'd looked terrified. *Was it a wild animal? A lion? What was he doing in the forest?*

The dense thicket of trees ahead of them thinned to reveal a sight that only a few from the outside world had ever seen. Towering structures loomed up out of the forest.

They weren't just skyscrapers. They curved and swooped, twisted and turned, and seemed to defy the laws of physics. Sunlight shone off steel and metal surfaces, sending shards of light into the surrounding woods. It would be a strange picture for someone unfamiliar with the landscape—a futuristic city rising up out of a jungle—but this was no ordinary place. It was Wakanda, the most technologically advanced nation on the face of the earth, and it was ruled by T'Chaka, the Black Panther and King of Wakanda. This was the Golden City.

The Dora Milaje paused in front of the Royal Palace, their spear points lowered to the ground. The palace rose up out of the ground like a great orb, with a single door framed in gold and jade. Darkness beckoned from within. T'Challa turned to look at M'Baku, then both boys stepped through.

T'Challa's footsteps echoed in his ears. The floors were black jade and highly polished, casting a shadowy reflection back up at him. A massive slab of obsidian carved into the shape of a panther crouched at the far end of the room, ready to pounce. Its color was beyond black—a lustrous, inky hue that had no equal. The eyes were its most intimidating feature—two red gemstones that seemed to pierce T'Challa's very soul. When he was a child, he was afraid of those eyes, but now he saw them as a reminder of his nation—strong and always alert.

Up ahead, his father sat on the Panther Throne, its

surface studded with gleaming stones and rare metals. The throne would someday be T'Challa's—*if* he could pass the grueling tests and gain the ceremonial title of Black Panther.

His father seemed to take up all the air in the room. Just his presence alone was enough to make grown men bow their heads in reverence. He wore the robes and heraldry of the Panther Tribe, and his garments shifted in color as T'Challa approached.

But his father wasn't alone.

M'Baku's father, N'Gamo, who sat on the king's war council, stood next to him.

M'Baku bowed his head as he stood before his king, then glanced at his father, who remained motionless, like a soldier carved from wood.

The King of Wakanda rose from his throne. He was a big man, broad-shouldered and strong, and the weight of the nation rested on his shoulders.

"Son," he began. "M'Baku. Where have you been?"

The torches in the wall flickered, as if his voice were strong enough to extinguish them.

T'Challa swallowed. His mouth was dry. "In the forest, Father. Playing games. I finished my studies and all of my lessons are complete."

The king nodded slowly. He eyed M'Baku, and then his gaze drifted back to T'Challa. "I have called you here because there is trouble brewing in the kingdom."

N'Gamo finally stirred. "My spymaster has received troubling reports of unknown invaders on our borders. We have intercepted some of their transmissions."

T'Challa's heart skipped. "We saw a strange man. He wasn't from Wakanda. He was injured by an animal. Is he . . . one of them?"

"He will be questioned," the Black Panther replied, "and we will certainly find out."

N'Gamo gave a grim smile.

"Who are they?" T'Challa asked. "Where are they from?"

The Black Panther glanced at M'Baku briefly before returning his gaze to T'Challa. "I will tell you, in time. But for now, you must stay safe. If war is on the horizon, I will not put your life at risk. So I am sending you away, for the time being."

T'Challa swallowed nervously. Surely he was hearing things.

"You will join him," N'Gamo said to M'Baku. "Perhaps the two of you can keep an eye on each other, and not get into too much trouble."

T'Challa pulled at his collar, but before he could ask another question, M'Baku asked it for him. "Where?" he said timidly, averting his gaze from the king. "Where will we be going?"

The king sat down. A ring shone on his finger, a simple

silver band, but T'Challa knew it was much more than that. "I have associates in America," he said. "I know a place where you will both be safe."

America, thought T'Challa. He had heard of the distant land, but Wakandans seldom traveled there, preferring never to leave their kingdom. Everything they needed was right here, including the source of their wealth and livelihood—Vibranium.

T'Challa cast a furtive at glance at M'Baku, who seemed to have frozen where he stood. "*Where* in America?" he asked.

"You will be going to Chicago," his father replied.

T'Challa cocked an eyebrow. "Chicago?" He tried to recall anything he had heard about the city, but came up blank.

"Yes," the Black Panther answered.

"We have enrolled you both at a school," N'Gamo said. "South Side Middle School. You must assume new identities."

T'Challa's head spun.

"A regular school?" he ventured. "With regular *kids*?"

"I have many enemies," the king said. "And I will not have them know of your whereabouts. Therefore, you will be posing as exchange students from Kenya. My friends at the African Embassy of Nations will be your cover."

T'Challa frowned, but tried to not let his dismay show. What his father said was true. He was used to being wary all his life. The kidnapping of a young prince could make a determined criminal very rich. If, he thought, his father didn't destroy them first.

"You will leave in a few days' time," the king said. "But first, we will have a feast in your honor."

Chicago, T'Challa thought, and finally remembered something he'd heard about the city.

It was said to be very cold there.

CHAPTER THREE

"America!" M'Baku whisper-shouted as they left the Royal Palace. "Can you believe it?"

"So you *want* to go?" T'Challa asked.

M'Baku paused midstep. "Of course I want to go! We'll be able to do anything we want, whenever we want."

M'Baku did have a point, T'Challa realized. But they'd have to hide their identities. That wouldn't be too much fun.

"Ah, I get it," M'Baku said, crossing his arms and smirking. "You won't get the royal treatment over there because no one'll know who you are. You'll have to live like us commoners. No one waiting on you hand and foot."

T'Challa was struck.

Was that it? Was he a spoiled brat who couldn't bear the thought of living without all his privilege?

"That's not it," he said. "I want to go—but if Wakanda is under threat, I should be here, with my father, to fight by his side if it comes to that."

"Don't worry," M'Baku said. "You'll have plenty of time for fighting when you become the next Black Panther."

T'Challa paused. Late-afternoon light glinted off the mountains in the distance, and he felt the sun on his face. "That'll be a long time yet," he replied wistfully.

M'Baku clapped his friend on the back. "Enough talking," he said. "Want to race to the city square?"

T'Challa smiled. M'Baku was too competitive for his own good. "Go!" shouted the young prince.

After saying good night to M'Baku—who won the race again, to T'Challa's dismay—he made his way to his room, which was set apart from his father's royal quarters. Like everything in Wakanda, his room was a blend of high-tech wizardry fused with nature. His bed was large, with sheets and pillows made from fine fabrics; high-definition moving images of the Wakandan countryside were embedded on flat screens in the walls, and tribal sculptures sat on pedestals and small columns. Under his feet was a soft carpet of woven grass.

He sat on his bed and let out a sigh.

This was the only home he knew, and he loved it more

than anything in the world. The forests, the people, the very culture itself were all a part of him. A part of him he did not want to lose.

"Chicago," he said aloud, and then tapped a bead on his Kiyomo Bracelet. To an outsider, it would have looked like a simple string of black beads around his wrist. But to Wakandans, it was much more. At birth, every child was given a Kiyomo Bracelet to wear. Each bead had a purpose—from storing medical records to taking a picture or projecting a free-floating informational screen, much like a web page but suspended in midair.

T'Challa watched as thousands of tiny black dots swirled from the bead and knitted together to form an image of the Chicago skyline and lakefront. His black cat, Bast, appeared from the hallway and jumped onto the bed. She nudged him with her head, begging for a scratch behind the ears. T'Challa obliged. "I'm going to miss you, little one," he said. Bast purred deeply, stretching her neck against his fingers. For a moment, T'Challa's eyes watered, but he quickly coughed instead, and pretended it hadn't happened.

T'Challa turned back to the screen. In just a few minutes he learned that Chicago was famous for its sports teams, music, and food. The city was situated right on Lake Michigan and was known for its cold winters and strong, bone-chilling winds. That was certainly something he'd have to get used to. It was always sunny and warm in Wakanda.

He waved his hand through the image and it winked

out. Bast leapt from the bed and meowed. "Want to go for a walk?" T'Challa asked.

Outside, T'Challa raised his head to the night sky. A crescent moon shone brightly in a field of black, surrounded by gleaming stars. It was hot, like always, and he was glad for his loose-fitting clothes, which allowed the slight breeze to cool him off a little. Perhaps he would take a quick swim in the nearby pond, he thought, although rumor had it that a great crocodile prowled through the reeds there late at night, looking for the foolish victim who decided on a midnight swim.

Perhaps not, he decided.

Instead, he went to his favorite place, away from the bustle of the city center. He called it the oasis—a salt marsh surrounded by fragrant trees and flowering plants. He loved being among the African juniper and leopard orchids, the water hyacinths and sweet jasmine. Small creatures stirred in the brush, night birds whistled, and every now and then a lion roared in the distance.

T'Challa looked heavenward. He thought back to the stories his father had told him when he was a child. Thousands of years ago, his father had said, a great meteor crashed into Wakanda. Amid the smoking and burning debris, something was found—something that would change the future of their country.

It was an energy-absorbing metal that vibrated upon

closer inspection. The warriors of Wakanda crafted weapons from it and learned that it was stronger than any mineral, gemstone, or metal they had ever seen. They called it Vibranium.

But there was a downside.

The crash site was radioactive, and several Wakandans were supposedly turned into demon spirits. That was when the great warrior Bashenga prayed to the Panther God, Bast, for strength and defeated them. He became the first Black Panther, and his line led down through the ages to T'Challa's father and to him.

T'Challa let out a breath. There was another story his father told him, and it usually came to him when he was alone or feeling melancholy. It was of his mother, N'Yami, who died after bringing him into the world. She was a true Queen of Wakanda, his father had said, beautiful and strong. Sometimes T'Challa imagined her walking hand in hand with his father among their people, proud and loved by all.

I wish I had known you, Mother.

A rustling in the bushes made him turn. "Who's there?" he called.

All was quiet for a moment, until a figure appeared out of the woods surrounding the oasis.

"Thought I'd find you here . . . *brother.*"

T'Challa stiffened. "What are you doing here?"

Hunter approached him with a swagger. "I always know where to find you. You're as loud as an elephant."

T'Challa bristled. His older stepbrother was known as one of the best trackers in Wakanda, even at his young age.

"I know you're going away," Hunter continued. "Father told me."

He already knows?

Hunter smiled, and it was not friendly. "Don't worry. When the fighting starts, I'll be here by Father's side, not running off to hide in America."

T'Challa clenched his fists. His pulse raced. It was always like this with Hunter—each one-upping the other, trying to gain the king's favor.

"It's not my decision to go," T'Challa said. "If it were up to me, I'd stay. I'm not afraid to fight."

Hunter laughed and drew close to T'Challa, so that the two boys were facing each other, with only a few inches between them. Hunter's eyes were green, and they gleamed with a cold light. "Say whatever you like, little brother. But while you're away, I'll keep your royal seat warm for you."

And with that, he turned and disappeared back into the woods.

T'Challa fumed. The sting of his words cut deep. But that was what Hunter did best—getting under his skin. *I am Father's true son,* he thought. *Not you.*

He thought back to the story his father had told him

long ago. Hunter was an orphan, the only survivor of a plane crash in which his mother and father had died. Many Wakandans didn't accept him because of his white skin, but the king took him in and raised him as his own.

But you'll never be Black Panther, T'Challa thought. *I have the birthright, and the blood.*

T'Challa looked down. Bast was circling his legs, purring loudly. He reached down and picked her up, and returned to his room, Hunter's words still ringing in his ears.

CHAPTER FOUR

Over the next few days, T'Challa had a lot to do. He not only had to pack all his clothes—what did kids wear in America?—but he also had to finish his classes with his tutors. Being the son of the king meant that all his lessons were given privately in the Royal Palace. There were also the duties that came with being a prince. These were his least favorite, but there was no getting around them. *Matters of state*, his father called them.

Often, when his father had visitors, T'Challa had to put on formal clothes and stand by his father's side, as if he too were deciding important issues. This was not true, of course—it was only a display of unity on behalf of the royal family. M'Baku often ribbed him for all the praise and attention he received just for doing nothing. *Prince Lucky*, he called him. T'Challa usually brushed it off, but sometimes it really grated at him.

The news spread quickly through Wakanda that their prince was going away. His father called it a journey of discovery and said that his son would be traveling abroad to learn about the greater world. It seemed to T'Challa that the king didn't even want his own people to know his true whereabouts. How dangerous was this threat he had spoken of? He would have to ask before he left for America.

America.

He was reminded once again of the strangeness of it all. He just hoped that he and M'Baku would be able to fit in.

The day before the celebration, T'Challa and M'Baku took a walk through the city center. Preparations were underway. Open-air pavilions were being set up, and T'Challa marveled at the Wakandan artistry on display. Some structures were made from material that looked as thin as paper, but curved and folded into elaborate shapes. Some bore wide ribbons of red and yellow cloth formed into houselike structures and adorned at the top with great capstones. But the one that took his breath away was a pyramid that looked to be made of glass, sparkling in the sun.

"This is all for you, my friend," M'Baku said, waving a hand in the air.

"Well, you, too," T'Challa countered. "It's for both of us."

M'Baku frowned. "Right. Keep telling yourself that."

T'Challa shook his head. "Your father is a high-ranking military official. A close advisor to the king. Your well-being is just as important as mine."

M'Baku nodded along, and then his eyes brightened. "Hey, I have an idea. Maybe when we get to America, I'll be the prince and you can be the pauper."

"Very funny," countered T'Challa. "You're a real joker."

That night, T'Challa met his father at the palace to learn more about his trip. He entered the throne room as another man was leaving. He was clean-shaven and massive, with arms as big as tree trunks. He nodded respectfully at T'Challa and then left the room.

T'Challa listened to the man's footsteps as they faded down the hall. After waiting another moment, he flopped into one of the many chairs and stretched his legs out in front of him. He rubbed his forehead.

"Tired?" his father asked.

T'Challa looked up. "Not really. Just wondering what it'll be like in Chicago." He shifted in his seat. "Why did you choose it? Why not New York or another city?"

The Black Panther cradled his chin in his hands. "I spent time there when I was a young man, studying and learning about the world outside of Wakanda. I found the people there down-to-earth and honest. I think you will, too."

"I really want to see New York one day," T'Challa said.

His father nodded. "Chicago is cold, T'Challa, but New York can be even colder if one does not find his or her way. I'm sure you'll do well in the Windy City. Plus, the African Embassy of Nations knows who we are, and is making accommodations as we speak. You'll be in good hands."

"But what about this threat?" T'Challa challenged him. "I should be here. By your side . . . in case of war."

"A son's duty is to obey his father," the king said.

"What about Hunter?" T'Challa persisted. "He's staying. Why can't—"

"Hunter is not in line for the throne. He doesn't carry the blood of the Panther Tribe. You know this, T'Challa."

T'Challa studied his feet.

When the fighting starts, I'll be here by Father's side, not running off to hide in America.

"You have a different destiny, my son," the king declared. "It will do you some good to be away. If you're ever going to lead, you'll need to understand the hopes and dreams of people from all walks of life, from all over the world. It will make you a better leader when it is your time to rule."

T'Challa looked up at his father. His face seemed to be carved from onyx, every angle sharp and prominent. It was a stern face, but one that could easily break into a smile— although it was a rare thing. Fortunately T'Challa had seen it several times. "What about these invaders?" he asked. "Did you find out more?"

The king furrowed his brow. "I think it may be a man by the name of Ulysses Klaw, but I'm not certain. He is a rogue scientist, and has always wanted to get at our supply of Vibranium."

"Klaw," T'Challa whispered. "Where is he from? Is that who the prisoner works for? What will you do to him?"

The lines on the king's forehead grew deeper. "The less you know, the safer you will be for now, T'Challa."

T'Challa sank down in his chair. He was always left out of the more interesting stuff in the kingdom—the intrigue and political maneuverings. Why did his father treat him like a child?

"Now," his father said, steepling his fingers together, "enough talk of troubles. Are you up for a game of chess? One last match?"

"Sure," T'Challa said, sitting up. "I choose black."

CHAPTER FIVE

T'Challa heard the drumming first—a percussive *boom boom boom*, accented by bells, whistles, shakers, marimbas, and a balafon, an instrument similar to a xylophone. The music drifted up into a night sky filled with stars. This was more than just a tribal rhythm. It was rooted in the history of Wakanda—a song of the ancestors, and every note and chord had a meaning.

T'Challa released a labored breath. All day, his stomach had been fluttering like a swarm of bees. The time had finally arrived.

M'Baku stood next to him and swayed to the music. "Ready to party?" he asked.

T'Challa nodded absently.

"*Hello?*" M'Baku said.

T'Challa was brought back to the moment. "Yes," he said. "It's time. Let's do it."

"One for all and all for one, right?" M'Baku said.

"Right," T'Challa answered, as they made their way down into the gathered masses.

The boys walked up a small hill, which looked down into a valley where the festivities were being held. Torches planted every few feet flickered orange in the dark. T'Challa felt the vibration of the music dance along his spine. A sea of people moved in an undulating rhythm—thousands of them, all in their traditional clothing, which made for a dazzling array of color—ruby red and emerald green, pure violet and lemony yellow. T'Challa stood and took it all in. Troubadours, jugglers, dancers, singers—even magicians came out to perform for the children in attendance. The Wakandan flag waved from every vantage point—a panther's proud face on a field of red, black, and green.

But amid the lavish display, T'Challa felt a sense of unease. He saw the preparations for a possible invasion in the fortifications of steel and concrete around the city entrances. Sharpshooters perched on soaring antenna towers. Squadrons of warriors patrolled the streets, and the number of Dora Milaje seemed to have doubled over the past few days.

A storm of applause broke out when the crowd spotted T'Challa. He wanted to disappear. He'd asked his father if he could arrive in his own way, without fanfare, and the king reluctantly allowed it, but all the cheering still put him in the spotlight. Cries of "Prince!" and "Young Panther!" rang throughout the valley.

M'Baku rolled his eyes, and as a new melody drifted out over the crowd, he pushed his friend into the throng. T'Challa quickly righted himself. He was not very good at dancing, but as several people circled him, he had no choice but to try his best. He felt awkward on his feet, which was strange, as he was usually one of the most physically capable boys in the kingdom. But this was dancing, something entirely alien to him. Still, for a few brief moments, his hesitation about his trip seemed to leave him.

Until he saw a lone figure leaning against a column, smirking.

Hunter shook his head. "Ah, the young prince is a good dancer," he called.

T'Challa broke away from the crowd and approached his stepbrother. "You don't know when to stop, do you?"

Hunter lifted his arms and gestured at the festivities held in T'Challa's honor. "All this is for you, little brother. But you don't deserve it. Kings do not run away."

Pinpricks stung the back of T'Challa's neck. "I'm not running away. I'm only obeying my king." He thought back to what his father had said: *A son's duty is to obey his father.*

Hunter shook his head very slowly, as if in disgust. "Call

it what you like, but everyone knows what it really is. You're afraid, T'Challa. Just admit it. You'll feel better once you get it off your chest."

Anger welled up inside of T'Challa. He clenched his fists. He was tired of the insults.

Hunter stood with his arms crossed. A few of his friends lurked behind him, as if they were his own private security force. "Perhaps you should get back to your dancing," Hunter taunted him. "You know, stick to what you're good at."

T'Challa snarled and dropped to a crouch, then spun on his heel, sweeping Hunter's legs out from under him.

Hunter shot back up and swung wildly, missing T'Challa by inches, giving the young prince the chance to drive his fist into Hunter's stomach. The music trailed off, and the crowd began to sense the commotion as the two boys circled each other.

T'Challa blew a breath through his nostrils and charged into Hunter, wrestling him to the ground. They were a tangle of arms and legs, kicking, punching. The crowd grew and began to shout.

T'Challa spun out from under Hunter and quickly bounded to his feet. Hunter rose just as fast, ready for another strike.

"Enough!"

T'Challa froze.

There was only one voice that strong, and T'Challa knew who it belonged to.

He watched his father, the King of Wakanda, rise from his seat. He stood between two panther statues and crossed his arms. Silence fell immediately. Then, with a simple wave of his hand, the king called for the music to begin again.

T'Challa and Hunter approached their father without having to be called, as if they were still children. Both boys were winded, their breaths coming in short bursts.

The king looked at his sons with smoldering eyes. "You are too old for this," he said. "I will have no more of it. Do you understand?"

"He insulted me," T'Challa spat out. "He—"

The king raised his hand, and T'Challa bit back his anger.

"Apologize to Hunter, T'Challa," the king demanded.

T'Challa couldn't believe it. "I didn't even start it!"

A muscle along the hard edge of the king's jaw twitched.

T'Challa sighed, then turned and offered his hand. "I'm sorry," he said curtly.

The king looked to Hunter. "You are not blood. But you are bound by family. Apologize to your brother, Hunter."

Hunter looked as if he wanted to strangle T'Challa, but instead reached out a hand with fake sincerity. "Sorry, little brother. I was in the wrong. Please accept my apology."

T'Challa grasped his hand, and, as much as he wanted

to crush it, gave it a firm grip instead. "Apology accepted," he said.

"Now," the king said. "This is supposed to be a celebration. I want you both to enjoy the rest of the night. No more fighting. Understood? You must put on a good face for our people."

The boys traded venomous glances and turned to leave.

"T'Challa," the king called.

T'Challa turned around, and his father nodded to a seat at his table, overflowing with food. Hunter gave one more withering glance and disappeared into the crowd. The Dora Milaje stood close by, like statues, but ones that could spring to life in an instant.

The Black Panther sat down, and T'Challa joined him. For a long moment the king only stared at his son. "What happened?" he finally asked.

T'Challa wanted to put it behind him, but the words fell from his mouth too quickly. "He says I'm a coward. That I'm running away to hide. He says that I should stay and fight."

He lowered his head and studied his hands.

The king nodded. "Many men will try to battle you with words, T'Challa, but words cannot sway a man from his duty."

T'Challa sighed. His father always spoke in riddles. "So I should just ignore him, then?"

"A wise man would," the king answered. "You have a strong will and mind, but Hunter is rash. He doesn't think ahead. That is why you will be king someday."

Hearing his father speak, T'Challa was reminded of his destiny. If he was going to be King of Wakanda one day, he had to act like it. "I will try my best, Father," he said.

The music was in full swing again, and the crowd was back to dancing and celebrating.

"I have some things for your trip," the king said, lightening the moment.

He reached down to the side of his seat and pulled out a black box encrusted with gemstones. It clicked open on silent hinges. "Here are several things you will need if you are ever in an emergency."

T'Challa peered inside the velvet-lined box. At first he didn't see anything, but after a moment, something seemed to shimmer like black mercury, with hints of silver running throughout it. *Only one thing looks like that,* he thought. *But it can't be.* He wasn't ready.

His father reached in and pulled out a length of fabric that unfurled like a black wave. T'Challa's eyes widened. It was a suit, just like his father's. The suit of the Black Panther.

The king noticed his son's surprise. "It was made by a team of my most brilliant scientists. It doesn't have all the properties of the one I wear, but still, it will protect you in an emergency."

"But I thought the suit was only to be worn by the ruling Black Panther," T'Challa said in amazement. "What about the heart-shaped herb? Will I take that with me also?"

The king almost laughed. "No, my son. It will destroy your mind and body if you are not prepared."

T'Challa knew the heart-shaped herb was the last test one had to undertake to rise as the Black Panther. After several daunting tasks, the juices from the herb were applied to the candidate's body, giving him superhuman strength, extrasensory skills, and the endurance to take on any foe.

"That day will come," his father explained. "But for now, I think we can make an exception, yes?" T'Chaka handed the suit to his son. The young prince took it reverently. The material was black and supple, stronger than leather and softer than silk.

"It is lined with Vibranium," T'Chaka said, "and will protect you from many dangers."

T'Challa felt hypnotized by the suit. It was one piece, and he was sure it would fit him like a glove. There was a mask, too, that he could wear over his eyes. He couldn't wait to put it on.

Something within the young prince began to take shape. It was a deep pull that he felt within his whole body, like a tide washing into shore. He had felt it before, and now he knew what it was—the call to adventure.

"T'Challa?"

T'Challa raised his head.

"Do not wear it unless you are in an emergency. Do you understand?"

T'Challa nodded absently, still mesmerized by the strange material.

"Here," his father said. "There is one more thing you should see."

He reached back within the box. T'Challa's heart hammered. *What else?*

The king handed him the object. It was a ring. A gleaming jewel sat in the center of it, like a cat's eye.

"I had this crafted especially for you, T'Challa. A Vibranium ring, a reminder of home."

T'Challa felt the weight of it in his palm and slipped it on his finger.

"The ring will fit a true son of Wakanda," his father said proudly. "And that is what you are."

T'Challa extended his fingers and looked admiringly at the ring, which sparkled in the torchlight.

"Remember that, my young prince, always."

"I will, Father."

"T'Challa," his father said, and his voice took on a grave tone. "Use the Panther suit only if there is no other choice. Do you understand?"

"I do."

"Good. Now, run and find M'Baku. Your plane leaves in the morning."

T'Challa studied the ring on his finger once more, then

looked out at the crowd from the vantage point of his father's table, set high above the celebration. *A true son of Wakanda,* he thought. *That is who I am. I will lead these people one day, no matter what Hunter says.*

He made a vow never to forget it.

CHAPTER SIX

T'Challa looked out from the plane's window. The landscape was as vibrant as a painting. From this high up, he could still make out the glimmering spires and ornamental architecture of the Golden City.

The plane was piloted by J'Aka, one of his father's top advisors. It was a state-of-the-art machine equipped with so much technology it made the young prince's head spin: infrared sensors, X-ray lasers, spotlights, gyroscopes, gun turrets, and high-tensile wire nets that could be released from a hatch to ensnare and capture enemies.

The quiet motion of the plane put him at ease. Two flight attendants were there to cater to his every whim. All he had to do was push a button. On the tray next to him was a bottle of water from a Wakandan spring, and a phone/search device that would have been the envy of Silicon Valley if they'd known it existed. He leaned back and basked in the moment, realizing it might be a while before he could enjoy life's little luxuries again.

"Wake up."

T'Challa groggily opened his eyes but then closed them again.

"T'Challa. We're almost there. Wake up."

He sat up, completely unaware of where he was. M'Baku leaned over him, just inches from his face. T'Challa's breath came short. Something was wrong. *I can't breathe!*

"Achooo!"

"Got you!" M'Baku roared, as a peanut flew from T'Challa's nostril.

"Very funny," T'Challa said. "I'm so glad you came along." He tossed the peanut into the wastebasket next to him.

"What would you do without me?" M'Baku asked.

Breathe a little easier, T'Challa thought.

M'Baku nudged T'Challa aside and looked through the window. "Look at all those cars," he said. "I think I'll buy one when we get there."

"With what money?" T'Challa teased, pushing him away. "How much did your father give you?"

"Probably not enough," M'Baku said. "But I can always get more from you, right?"

T'Challa shook his head. M'Baku's father was strict and wasn't one to afford his son luxuries.

T'Challa yawned and pressed his nose against the window. The blue ribbon of Chicago's lakefront came into view, bordered by a massive highway. Cars as small as ants sped along it.

"I think I'm going to do quite well here," M'Baku said, crossing his arms behind his head and leaning back against the leather headrest. "We're from Wakanda. What does America have that we don't?"

His friend had a point. Wakanda led the world in science, physics, robotics, weapons research, and much more. But they were going to be strangers in a strange land. There would definitely be a steep learning curve. T'Challa closed his eyes again.

Soon, they touched down at a private airfield. T'Challa assumed it was private, as there was no one else around except for an older man who greeted J'Aka as an old friend. From there, they were driven to the embassy.

T'Challa's father had set them up at the African Embassy of Nations on Michigan Avenue, right in the heart of the city. They were to take their dinners in their rooms, and the staff was not to speak of their visit. Every day, they would have to take a bus to school, to keep up appearances. After all, they couldn't be dropped off in a limousine with tinted windows and an armed driver.

J'Aka maneuvered the sleek black car along the highway as if he had done it a thousand times. T'Challa looked out of the window. At first, all he saw were fields and farms, but slowly, the traffic became more congested. Buildings rose up like wild things, steel and concrete towers wreathed in fog. It was different from Wakanda, T'Challa realized. There wasn't enough green. The words *concrete jungle* came to mind.

People were everywhere—walking on the streets, bundled up in big coats, heads tucked against the wind. T'Challa shivered. Just moments before, when they'd landed at the airfield, they were led through a tunnel to their car without even venturing into the open air, but he still felt the drop in temperature. He had to admit, he wasn't looking forward to Chicago's legendary cold.

Finally, they arrived on a street where shops with lighted windows and artistic fashion displays lined both sides. "The Magnificent Mile," J'Aka pointed out.

M'Baku peered out the window. "I've heard of this," he said. "This is where all the rich people shop!"

T'Challa shook his head.

The car passed a very plain-looking brick building nestled between two larger ones. "Here we are," J'Aka announced. He parked in an underground garage and then led both boys to the lobby and front desk. He disappeared into the back with a man wearing a Bluetooth earpiece. T'Challa took a moment to look around. The ceiling was high, with several gleaming chandeliers, but the carpet was brown and a little soiled. The wooden furniture was old and unpolished. "Some embassy," M'Baku groaned.

A moment later, J'Aka returned. A young man wearing a cap and black suit followed him and piled their luggage onto a cart. He looked at T'Challa and M'Baku with curiosity.

"The concierge will show you to your room, and then I will be on my way back," J'Aka said. "Your father said to tell you one more time to be on your best behavior." He looked at both boys. "Understood?"

They both nodded. J'Aka shook their hands, gave a small nod to T'Challa, then departed.

The embassy room was small, with two beds, a tiny refrigerator, a smaller bathroom, and drab brown curtains.

"We have to share a room?" M'Baku complained.

"I don't think we're in Wakanda anymore," T'Challa replied.

M'Baku shook his head. "You're a prince and you're gonna live like this?"

"Shh!" T'Challa whispered, and then knocked on a thin wall. "People could hear us. I have to remain secret, remember?"

"Yeah," said M'Baku, throwing his bag on the floor. "I hear you."

T'Challa found a safe in the closet and immediately came up with a combination, then tucked the box with his suit and ring inside. He looked around the room. One small window let in weak gray light.

"Oh," he heard M'Baku call with curiosity. "This is interesting."

T'Challa walked over to see what it was. M'Baku knelt on one knee next to an open cabinet under a small refrigerator. T'Challa lowered his head and looked inside. He smiled. It was a treasure trove of American snacks arranged in neat little rows: potato chips, chocolate, crackers, popcorn, nuts, chewing gum, more chocolate, and several things he didn't even recognize.

M'Baku raised an eyebrow. "Hungry?"

Twenty minutes later both boys were spread out on their separate beds holding their stomachs. M'Baku had even eaten all the breath mints. "I think I'm going to be sick," he groaned.

T'Challa had eaten his fair share, too. Wakanda was not known for junk food, and both boys were hungry from their flight. His father would certainly not have approved. He lay back and put a hand over his stomach. "I think it was the extra candy bar that pushed me over the edge," he said.

And then he belched.

A loud rattle sounded in his ears. He turned his head. M'Baku was already asleep, snoring like a rhino.

CHAPTER SEVEN

BEEP. BEEP. BEEP. BEEP...

T'Challa jumped up and peered around the room. For a moment, he didn't know where he was, until it all came rushing back to him.

I'm in America.

Chicago.

I'm going to school here.

M'Baku grimaced. "What in the name of the Panther God is that racket?"

T'Challa followed the sound to a clock on the bedside table. The red digital numbers flashed 7:00 A.M. He knew he hadn't set it. Someone from the embassy must have programmed it earlier. He hit the OFF button.

Knock. Knock. Knock.

"Who's that?" M'Baku said warily.

"I guess we better find out," T'Challa replied.

He got up and threw on one of the fluffy robes he'd retrieved from the closet. "Coming," he called, pulling the robe around him.

He opened the door as M'Baku ducked into the bathroom. T'Challa was met by a man in a black butler's uniform standing behind a cart stacked with silver trays and pitchers of water and juice. "Breakfast is served, sirs."

T'Challa stepped aside, and the man rolled his cart onto the hardwood floor. As T'Challa watched, the man made a very slow display of uncovering every dish with a flourish. After he left, M'Baku came out of the bathroom with wet hair. "What is that?" he asked, rubbing a towel on his head.

T'Challa lifted one of the round metal domes. "Breakfast?"

M'Baku came closer, peering at the food. "What are Yummy Flakes?" he asked, pointing to a box displaying a smiling boy with a spoon in his mouth.

T'Challa tore open the box and looked at the small flakes of what looked like shredded tree bark. "I don't know," he said, and popped a few pieces in his mouth. His face soured. "Yick," he said.

"Let me try it," M'Baku offered.

He took a handful, threw back his head and poured a bunch of flakes down his throat. He chewed for a second, considering, and then downed a glass of milk. "Not bad," he said.

T'Challa surveyed the tray again. He was confused. There were several round pieces of fried bread, but they had holes in the middle. Some were dark and some were light, and some were sprinkled with little colored dots. "Looks like they don't have a very good bread maker here," M'Baku said. "They can't even make bread without putting a hole in it."

"I've seen these before," T'Challa said. "It's called a donut. I saw it in an American movie."

"Doe-*what*?" M'Baku asked skeptically.

T'Challa picked one up. He took a bite and chewed. "Pretty good," he said after a minute. "Tastes like chocolate."

M'Baku eyed a donut with sprinkles. "Here goes," he said, and stuffed the whole thing in his mouth. He looked at T'Challa as he chewed, and then, with great effort, swallowed loudly. His face suddenly went pale. "Uh-oh," he said.

"What?" asked T'Challa.

"My stomach hurts again."

A half hour later—after M'Baku had made several visits to the bathroom—the boys headed to the lobby. Men and women in business suits walked with purpose down the long corridors. People sat at tables in the lobby with their laptops open in front of them. T'Challa hadn't made eye contact with anyone since they'd arrived. Everyone's heads were buried in their phones.

A man stood behind the counter tapping away at a keyboard. He looked up, and his eyes widened. "Ah, I see you're ready for school. Was your room to your liking?"

He must know who we are, T'Challa thought. "Yes," he answered. "Thank you."

The man, whose glasses rested on his nose, turned to M'Baku. "Are you okay, young man?"

M'Baku swallowed. "Yeah. I . . . um . . . had too much sweet stuff."

The man nodded. "I see. Well, the snack bar is refilled every night, but you don't have to eat it all." He leaned over the counter and lowered his voice. "I do understand the temptation, though."

M'Baku didn't answer, just slowly bobbed his head. T'Challa couldn't help but snicker.

"Now," the concierge said, straightening back up and pointing over the boys' heads. "Through the revolving door and then across the street. You'll want the number 134 bus to the South Side." He clacked on his computer, and two small cards slid out of a black box. "These are bus passes. They're loaded up with fare money to get you around the city. Let me know when they run short."

He slid the cards across the smooth counter.

"Dinner will be served in your room at seven p.m. every

night. If you need anything at all, just let me know." He pointed to his name tag.

T'Challa leaned in. "Thank you, Clarence," he said.

M'Baku groaned, but still managed a half smile.

"I hope we didn't miss the bus," T'Challa said, rubbing his arms and craning his neck to see down the street. He shivered. Neither one of the boys had winter coats. How could someone have forgotten to get them coats? Perhaps Clarence at the embassy could give them some. They certainly wouldn't be able to make it through the Chicago winter without them.

Michigan Avenue was a bustle of activity. Buses, cars, motorcycles, pedestrians, bicycles—T'Challa even saw a kid on a skateboard—all fought for the fastest and least-congested lanes and sidewalks. M'Baku looked up at one of the tallest buildings, its pinnacle lost in white fog. "Well," he said. "It's definitely a big city, but Wakanda is more . . ." He paused, searching for the right word.

"Captivating?" T'Challa ventured.

"Exactly," M'Baku answered. "Captivating."

That *was* the right word, T'Challa realized. Even though Chicago was big, it couldn't match the grand elegance of Wakanda, with its dazzling architecture and unique culture. For a brief moment, he thought of his father. *Does he miss me yet? Or is his mind occupied with the possible threat from Ulysses Klaw?*

T'Challa looked down the street again. He did a double take.

There, in the center of all the rushing pedestrians on the sidewalk, a man was standing completely still. He stood out because of his height, and the military beret he wore did nothing to make him blend in.

And he was looking directly at T'Challa.

He reached out to nudge M'Baku, but his attention was startled by a creaking, groaning sound. A blue-and-white city bus with the number 134 pulsing in a weak orange light above the massive windshield was headed in his direction.

"That must be for us," M'Baku said.

The bus pulled up to the curb and released a hiss. A door flew open. T'Challa glanced down the street again, but the man had vanished. He placed his foot on the little step, and was immediately jostled and bumped by a horde of people getting off. They looked at him with annoyed faces.

"Great," said M'Baku.

The boys took a step back and waited as passengers got off, then made their way onto the bus. T'Challa took out the card Clarence had given him and handed it to the bus driver.

The driver, a big man with a beard, looked at T'Challa and raised an eyebrow. "Can I help you, young man?"

"Yes," T'Challa replied. "We're going to South Side Middle School. I think this card has our bus money on it."

The man closed his eyes and then opened them again slowly.

"Son," he said, "touch the card against the reader."

T'Challa looked down and saw a round column with a flat surface on top.

"What's the holdup?" M'Baku complained behind him, peeking over T'Challa's shoulder.

T'Challa placed the card on the reader.

BEEP.

"There you go," the driver said.

T'Challa turned to find a seat. Everyone on the bus was staring at him. He gulped. Fortunately for M'Baku, T'Challa had already embarrassed himself trying to pay his fare, so he didn't have to suffer the same fate.

Men and women in business suits stood in the aisle, their attention now back to their cell phones. It seemed that every seat was taken, either by a person, a bookbag, or a briefcase. T'Challa noticed several kids his age, fiddling with their phones and not talking to each other.

M'Baku was the first one to find a seat, and sat next to a girl wearing headphones who only stared out of the window. T'Challa looked left and right as he continued down the aisle. The bus came to a stop and he flew forward, barely righting himself. As he did, he saw that the seat in front of him was empty. "Is this seat available?" he asked.

A small, skinny boy looked up from the graphic novel he was reading. "What's that?"

"I asked if anyone is sitting here," T'Challa said.

The boy looked at the empty seat and then back to T'Challa. "Uh, nope," he said.

T'Challa slid into the seat. The bus lurched and he flew forward again. He sighed. He wasn't even at school yet, and he felt like he'd already been through an ordeal.

T'Challa sat and watched as more passengers got on—mostly businesspeople, but he also saw lots of teenagers, most of them with backpacks and wearing headphones. The seat was uncomfortable, and every bump and jolt made it even worse. They sat in traffic for what seemed like hours. A blast of heat came through the vents, and T'Challa felt sweat on his back. He turned to the boy next to him. "Hi, um. This bus goes to South Side Middle School, right?"

The boy slid his glasses up on his nose with one finger. "Yeah. It's like this every morning. Total bummer."

T'Challa didn't know what the boy meant.

"Are you new here?" the boy asked. He nodded in the direction of M'Baku. "I've never seen you or your friend before."

"Oh," T'Challa said. "Yes, we're new."

"I'm Ezekiel," the boy said. "Actually, everyone calls me Zeke."

T'Challa froze.

What's my name? Father said to keep my identity a secret, but he never gave me an alias!

T'Challa fidgeted in is seat. "I'm, uh . . ."

Think! he shouted inside his head. "I'm T.," he blurted out. "T. Charle—"

"Oh. Hey, T. Charles," Zeke replied.

T'Challa sighed a breath of relief. *T. Charles,* he thought. *Not bad.*

After a bumpy ride on the city streets, the Magnificent Mile was left behind, and the bus continued on to the South Side. They passed fast-food restaurants, electronics stores, check-cashing places, and what seemed like a hundred pawn shops. Finally, the bus pulled into a neighborhood with large homes on both sides of the street. After a few more turns, the bus wheezed and came to a stop. Everyone except the adults filed out. T'Challa looked through the window. "Where's the school?"

"Just around the corner," Zeke said. "This is the closest stop. C'mon. I'll show you the way."

"Oh," T'Challa said. "Okay. Thanks."

He found M'Baku in the crowd and they exited together. A minute or two later, T'Challa stood on the cracked sidewalk and took in his surroundings. South Side Middle School was a giant old mansion covered in ivy. Several small brick buildings fanned out from a larger one with a massive clock tower. The whole place was bordered by a fence. T'Challa couldn't help but think of a prison he had seen in Wakanda. There was only one, and it was reserved for the worst offenders and enemies of the king.

"C'mon," Zeke said. "Let me show you where to go." He led T'Challa and M'Baku into the school.

As soon as the door was opened, T'Challa was assaulted by a symphony of noise: metal lockers clanging shut, students shouting at the tops of their lungs, and teachers pleading for quiet. Most noticeable of all, though, was the music, which seemed to reverberate along his bones. At least, T'Challa *thought* it was music. He had never heard anything like it in his life. A few words drifted from one boy's portable radio, a massive box with two speakers:

I'm cooler than ice
And twice as nice
Watch me flow
Down real low
Like Curly and Moe.

T'Challa suddenly remembered that his father said there was something they should do right away when they arrived at the school. "We're supposed to meet the principal," he said to Zeke.

Zeke's eyes widened, looking from T'Challa to M'Baku. "You *want* to see the principal? On purpose?"

"Yeah," M'Baku piped up.

Zeke raised an eyebrow. "Okay," he said hesitantly.

T'Challa and M'Baku traded wary glances.

Zeke led them both to an office with a frosted-glass window that read PRINCIPAL. Inside, a man with glasses sat behind a desk, typing on a computer. "Good morning, Ezekiel," he said with a smile. His teeth were very straight and white, T'Challa noticed. "How can I help you today?"

Zeke stepped forward. "This is T.," he said, pointing to T'Challa. "T. Charles." He turned to M'Baku. "And this is his friend—"

M'Baku swallowed.

"Marcus," T'Challa said, coming to his rescue.

M'Baku nodded along, relieved. T'Challa wasn't sure if he needed an alias or not, and they hadn't even thought to talk about it.

"Ah," the man said, his eyes lighting up. "The exchange students from Kenya?"

"Uh, right," T'Challa stammered.

"I'm Mr. Walker," the man said. "Mrs. Deacon's assistant." He studied them both for a moment. "My wife and I were in Kenya last year. Beautiful country. Where, exactly—"

"We really need to see the principal," M'Baku cut in. "For our class schedules?"

"Ah," Mr. Walker said, glancing at his watch. "Yes, it is getting on in the morning. I'll let her know."

"Thank you," T'Challa said.

▲ ▲ ▲

The principal, Mrs. Deacon, was a tall woman with close-cropped hair and quick, birdlike eyes. T'Challa studied the rules she had just gone over with them:

- No one allowed in the halls during class without a pass
- No food or soda except in the cafeteria
- No bullying
- No chewing gum
- No music (which T'Challa thought strange, considering all the music he'd heard in the hallway)

Mrs. Deacon printed out their class schedules, and T'Challa looked at all the subjects: Advanced English, Social Studies, French—which he was already fluent in—Art Exploration, Advanced Sciences, Physical Education, and several more classes.

M'Baku stared at the list, aghast. "All of those?" he whispered, but loud enough for Mrs. Deacon to hear.

"Oh yes," she said. "That's just first semester."

M'Baku gulped.

CHAPTER EIGHT

T'Challa opened the door to the embassy room. "I'm exhausted," he said as he stepped inside and closed the door behind him.

"Tell me about it," M'Baku agreed. "I feel like I just ran thirty miles in the forest."

"The jet lag should wear off soon," T'Challa replied. "My father said we should stay up as late as we can the first few nights to get acclimated."

"Hey," M'Baku said. "What's this?"

Several shopping bags had been placed on both boys' beds. T'Challa picked up a note card on the pillow.

Thought you boys might need some Chicago gear.
—Clarence

"Clarence?" M'Baku asked.

"The concierge," T'Challa reminded him.

"Oh, right," said M'Baku.

They tore into the bags and found winter coats, thick socks, T-shirts, wool caps, and gloves. After a lot of back-and-forth, they both settled on the pieces they liked most.

"Now we're ready for Chi Town," M'Baku said, posing in front of the mirror.

"We are," said T'Challa, but wondered exactly what that meant.

The first few days at South Side Middle School went by in a rush. T'Challa was swept up in a whirlwind—memorizing students' and teachers' names, finding the right classrooms, and getting oriented to a completely new environment.

"I can't believe we've got all this homework," M'Baku complained one night at the embassy. Books and papers were spread out all over his bed, along with several empty potato chip bags.

"We'll get used to it," T'Challa consoled him. "Just give it a little time."

"Easy for you to say," replied M'Baku.

T'Challa didn't have trouble with any of his classes. He

had learned a lot at his father's knee. And then there were his tutors, of course, who were well-versed in everything from ancient civilizations to advanced robotics.

"I'll help you," T'Challa offered. "What are you having trouble with?"

M'Baku screwed up his face. "Uh, everything?"

A few days later, T'Challa found himself sitting in his French class, poring over verbs and sentence structure. It was gray outside, and the room was cold. He wished he had brought a sweater.

"And who can give me the correct conjugation of the verb *to be*?" asked Mrs. Evans, the French teacher. She sat behind her desk and surveyed her students. The classroom fell silent, except for the sound of pencils tapping against wooden desks. T'Challa had already answered several of her questions, and now he had a choice to make: Should he give her the correct answer, or wait for someone else to give it a shot?

Silence.

T'Challa waited.

And waited.

Mrs. Evans sighed, and rested her chin on her fist.

T'Challa raised his hand.

Mrs. Evans's eyes lit up—something that happened every time he answered a question.

"Yes, Mr. Charles?"

T'Challa gave a little cough, a nervous habit he seemed to have picked up as soon as he arrived in America. "The verb *to be*," he began. "Present tense: *je suis, tu es, il est, nous sommes, vous êtes, ils sont.*"

Mrs. Evans shook her head in what T'Challa thought could only be admiration. "Your enunciation is excellent," she said. *"Très bien, Monsieur Charles. Merci."*

The smile fled from her face as she returned her gaze to the class. "As for the rest of you, study lesson number two again. We'll be having this same drill again tomorrow. Class dismissed. *À bientôt.*"

The silence was broken by scraping chairs and groans. T'Challa received a few sidelong glances and smirks as people left the room. He couldn't help that he'd learned French at an early age. It was the national language of several African nations, and his father's visiting dignitaries used it when they greeted him. It was something he had to learn, the duty of a prince.

"Nice job, T."

T'Challa turned. It was the girl from the bus—the one who had sat next to M'Baku on that first day.

"You're an exchange student, right?" she asked. "From Kenya?"

"Yes," T'Challa answered.

"I'm Sheila. I think you met my friend Zeke already."

"Oh, yes," T'Challa said. "Zeke. He helped me get started on my first day. Me and my friend . . . Marcus."

There was a moment of silence as students filed past them, all talking and jostling.

"What's school like in Kenya?" Sheila asked.

T'Challa studied her face for a moment. She had tiny freckles, nutmeg-brown skin, and long corkscrew curls. "Well, it's really different. It's a little bit more . . ." He searched for the right word but came up blank.

"Disciplined?" Sheila suggested.

"Yeah. That's it," T'Challa said.

Sheila turned to the sound of kids shouting. "It *is* a little rowdy here. So how'd you get so good at French, anyway?"

"Well, there are a lot of French speakers in Africa, so I learned when I was little."

"I wish I learned when I was a kid," Sheila said with a hint of envy. "Conjugating verbs is the bane of my existence."

T'Challa smiled. He could already tell that Sheila was definitely smart, someone he could become friends with.

"Actually," Sheila said, "I'm more into science. The natural sciences, to be exact."

"Ah, like energy and matter, right?"

"Sure, but don't forget biology and natural phenomena."

T'Challa was impressed. He'd heard that American students didn't like to study, but Sheila put that rumor to rest already. They stood in silence for a brief moment. "Well," T'Challa said. "It was good to meet you, Sheila."

"You, too," Sheila replied. "See ya around."

She's nice, T'Challa thought, as she walked away. Maybe it wouldn't be so bad at South Side Middle School after all.

A few minutes later, he wasn't so sure about that.

The gymnasium smelled like dirty socks.

It was large, with a high ceiling, from which hundreds of small lights shone down. Several banners hung from the walls, each showing a roaring tiger on a field of green and yellow. "Wildcats," T'Challa whispered.

"Seems like you'll fit in," M'Baku joked. "You know. Cat family."

T'Challa cut his eyes at him.

"I'm gonna show these kids how it's really done," bragged M'Baku, cracking his knuckles.

"How what's done?" T'Challa asked.

"I don't know. Whatever it is they think they're good at."

T'Challa laughed. M'Baku certainly wasn't lacking in confidence.

After getting changed into their gym clothes—courtesy of the embassy—T'Challa and M'Baku fell in with the rest of the boys, forming a line. A loud whistle blow brought the class to attention. A man who was built like a fire hydrant—short and squat but all muscle—walked down the line with a clipboard and surveyed the students. "New year, new recruits," he said. "Some of you won't be able to hack it. Some of you will cry, and some of you may faint. But believe me, when you leave here, you'll be better men for it."

There were a few muffled snickers, but the instructor ignored them. M'Baku shot T'Challa a glance and rolled his eyes.

"My name is Mr. Blevins," the instructor said. "And today, we're going to learn the fundamentals of one of the world's oldest sports." He paused. "Wrestling."

M'Baku smiled. He and T'Challa had wrestled from an early age, and the two of them were about equal in their skill.

"Now," Mr. Blevins said, "I'm going to show you a few basic moves. But first, I need a volunteer. Any takers?"

Silence.

The students dropped their heads and shuffled their feet, squeaking their sneakers on the hardwood floor. T'Challa was reminded of his French class.

He was never one to back down from a challenge. Being the son of a king meant he'd had to prove himself to boys who thought they were better than he was more times than once. He stepped forward. M'Baku gave him a grin. A few of the students eyed him with curiosity.

"The new boy," Mr. Blevins said in surprise, sizing T'Challa up. He glanced at his clipboard. "T. Charles. Well, Mr. Charles. Let's do this."

T'Challa gave a weak smile.

"Do you know the referee's position?" Mr. Blevins asked, tossing his clipboard to the floor.

"I do," said T'Challa, and dropped to his hands and

knees. It was one of the first things he learned in Wakanda. Mr. Blevins took the advantage position and knelt on one knee, then placed one arm around T'Challa's middle. He rested the other on his elbow.

"Now," Mr. Blevins said, his voice carrying through the gymnasium. "On three, Mr. Charles here is going to try to escape. Ready?"

T'Challa released a breath. "Ready."

"One . . ." Mr. Blevins counted off. "Two . . . three."

T'Challa spun around on his knees and flipped Mr. Blevins on his back, pinning him to the mat in less than five seconds.

A chorus of *ooohhh*s went up from the crowd.

Mr. Blevins's eyes were still wide when T'Challa rose from the mat. "Well," Mr. Blevins said, getting up with a wry smile. "I haven't been taken down like that in years. That was quite . . . um, effective, T. Did you learn that in Kenya?"

T'Challa paused. Everyone was staring at him. Whispers filled the gymnasium. His mouth was dry. "I did," he finally said. "My father taught me."

Mr. Blevins brushed off his knees. "And what does he do?"

T'Challa swallowed. "Um, a lot of stuff."

M'Baku covered his mouth with his hand, stifling a laugh.

"Ah," Mr. Blevins said. "Looks like you'll have a head

start on the rest of us, then." He turned and addressed the class. "That's what I call team spirit! Wildcat spirit!"

"Wildcat spirit!" the class shouted back.

T'Challa grinned inside. He was off to a good start. But as he turned around, he saw that one boy in particular was staring right at him.

And he was smirking.

CHAPTER NINE

Later that day, T'Challa sat with M'Baku, Sheila, and Zeke in the cafeteria. The clatter of trays combined with the activity of hundreds of students made T'Challa's ears ring.

"So," Sheila began, turning to T'Challa. "I heard you were a great fighter, and that you landed Mr. Blevins on his butt."

T'Challa swallowed hard. He didn't want people to think he was a bully or a fighter.

"Hmpf," M'Baku muttered. "I could've done that. T'Challa just went first. That's all."

"I hate sports," Zeke chimed in. "I'd rather read a book."

T'Challa grinned.

Sheila reached into a brown paper bag and took out

a cookie. M'Baku's eyes lit up. "Want to try one?"

"Don't do it," warned Zeke.

Sheila screwed up her face.

"Why?" asked M'Baku. "Something wrong with it?"

"There's *nothing* wrong with it," Sheila said. "It's totally fine."

"Yeah," Zeke shot back. "If you like *gluten-free*."

T'Challa observed this interaction with curiosity.

"It still *tastes* good," Sheila said.

"What's gluten-free?" T'Challa asked.

"Well," Sheila began. "Gluten's a protein that's in certain types of wheat and grain, like rye and barley. But if you can't digest that kind of stuff, you can eat foods that don't have it, or find substitutes."

M'Baku looked at the cookie like it had just turned into a toad.

"Go ahead," Sheila encouraged him. "Try it."

M'Baku raised the cookie up to the light. After a long moment, he bit into it.

T'Challa, Zeke, and Sheila waited.

M'Baku nodded. "Not bad," he finally said.

Sheila looked at Zeke with satisfaction.

T'Challa bit into his hamburger. He'd heard that the cafeteria food wasn't very good, but he liked it because it was different from what he had at home—which was usually vegetables, lean meats, and grains. Here at South Side Middle School, they had hot dogs and hamburgers and lasagna and something called Jell-O, which he loved.

Zeke reached in one of his notebooks and pulled out a piece of paper, then slid it across the table. T'Challa picked it up and read:

After-School Activities
CHESS CLUB MEETING
4–5 p.m.
Study Hall Room 101

T'Challa grinned. His father had taught him how to play chess when he was five years old. He said it was a great tool to learn patience and strategic thinking. He looked up from the paper. "Did you sign up?" he asked Zeke.

"Yeah," Zeke answered. "But I'm not that great." He turned to M'Baku. "What about you, Marcus?"

M'Baku slid a spoonful of beans into his mouth.

"*Marcus*," T'Challa said, elbowing him.

M'Baku raised his head, spoon still up to his mouth. "Oh," he said, looking at T'Challa. "Yes. That's me. Uh, what's the question?"

Sheila and Zeke traded glances.

"I asked," Zeke said slowly, "do you want to join the Chess Club?"

"No," said M'Baku. "I don't think so. I want to try basketball. I saw the Chicago Bulls on TV in Wakan—"

T'Challa sucked in a breath.

M'Baku eyed him quickly. "Um, on TV . . . yeah. I saw them on TV, and I want to give it a try."

Zeke opened his mouth to speak, but T'Challa turned to the sound of loud voices. A slim, lanky figure approached the table—it was the boy who had stared at him in Phys. Ed. after he took down Mr. Blevins. He was the tallest boy T'Challa had ever seen. Two other boys were with him. One was small and wiry, like a slithering snake; the other was bigger than T'Challa, with muscles that strained beneath his shirt. All three of them had one thing in common: they did not have kind eyes, something his father said to always look for in a person.

The tall boy sauntered up to T'Challa. He wore low-slung pants tucked into brown boots. A silver ring displaying a skull glinted on his finger. He narrowed his eyes at T'Challa and M'Baku. "So you two from Africa?" he asked, an edge to his voice.

T'Challa eyed him. *Best to remain friendly,* he thought. "Yes," he said. "We're from Kenya."

"Ever hunt any elephants or kill any tigers?"

M'Baku smirked. "We don't hunt animals for fun," he said.

The boy laughed, a deep rumble. His friends behind him followed his lead. "Well, what *do* you do, then?" he asked. "They have hip-hop over there?"

T'Challa had never heard the words before. "What is 'hip-hop'?"

The group of boys burst into laughter. T'Challa was reminded of hyena howls he'd heard back home.

"Dude," the tall boy said. "You don't know hip-hop? West Side Posse? Killa Krew?"

T'Challa was still lost. He had no idea what the boy was talking about.

"They probably listen to more interesting music," Zeke suggested. "You know. Like, *African* music?"

The tall boy's eyes shifted to the small figure of Zeke. "Whatup, nerd? Where's your coloring book?"

Zeke blew a breath through his nostrils. "They're graphic novels," he said, staring straight ahead and not meeting the tall boy's eyes.

"Whatever," the tall boy said. "We're outta here. See you around, Africa." He walked away the same way he had come, with a spring in his step and a cocky grin. His friends trailed behind him.

No one spoke for a moment.

"Who was that?" T'Challa finally asked.

"His name's Gemini Jones," Zeke said. "And he's a real pain."

"Sure is," Sheila added.

Zeke glanced in the direction of Gemini and his friends at their table, set back way in the corner, away from everyone else. "People are afraid of him 'cause he says he's a warlock."

"A warlock?" T'Challa questioned.

"Yeah," Sheila replied. "A male witch."

"There's no such thing as witches," said M'Baku.

"Well," said Zeke, "I just read a graphic novel called *Hex and Wrex*, and it's all about warlocks."

Sheila gave him a withering look. "Uh, that's called fiction."

"But truth is *stranger* than fiction," Zeke said, and then, looking over the tops of his glasses, "Dun . . . dun . . . dun!"

Sheila closed her eyes.

"What about the other guys?" T'Challa asked. "Who are they?"

"The skinny guy's Deshawn," Sheila said, "and the big muscle-head dude calls himself . . . wait for it . . . Bicep."

"Bicep?" T'Challa echoed.

"I know, *right*?" Sheila said.

M'Baku laughed.

"I'd keep away from them if I were you guys," Zeke said. "They're always picking fights and getting in trouble."

But T'Challa wasn't sure about that. He didn't like the way Gemini Jones spoke to him. Who did he think he was?

But there was nothing he could do about it. He had to keep his identity secret. He rested his chin in his hands and sighed. "So," he said. "What *is* hip-hop, anyway?"

Lunch hour passed quickly. T'Challa returned his tray and headed into the hallway with Zeke, Sheila, and M'Baku. A group of kids stood in a circle in the middle of the hall, staring at the floor.

M'Baku pointed. "What's going on there?"

They walked the few short steps and T'Challa heard several voices mingled together:

What is it?

It's freaking creepy, is what it is.

Who put it there?

T'Challa pushed through the crowd. At first he didn't know what he was looking at. But as he drew closer, it became clearer. It was a bundle of small broken branches, held together by string and placed so that it stood upright, like a tripod for a camera.

"What in the name of Zeus is that?" Zeke asked.

"Some kind of nest?" Sheila ventured.

T'Challa stepped forward and bent down to get a closer look.

"Okay, okay," a booming male voice called out. "Move it along."

T'Challa stood back up. A teacher was pushing his way through the throng. The crowd broke up quickly, still murmuring.

"What do you think it is?" M'Baku asked.

T'Challa shrugged. "Something to do with Halloween?"

M'Baku shook his head. "Maybe. I don't know. But we're in America. There's all kinds of weird stuff over here."

T'Challa took another doubtful look at the weird object. "Yeah," he said uneasily. "I guess so."

CHAPTER
TEN

The boys' first weekend finally arrived, and they were eager to get out and explore the city. They'd seen next to nothing besides their school and the embassy since they'd landed in Chicago.

"Where do you want to go?" M'Baku asked, tying his sneakers.

T'Challa hesitated. "I don't know. We should probably stay close, though, right?"

M'Baku let out an exasperated breath. "T'Challa, we can do anything we want! Who's gonna know?"

T'Challa thought about that. There was a whole city to explore. Were they supposed to stay in their rooms the whole time they were going to be here? "You're right," he confessed. "Let's do it."

But in the back of his mind, he heard his father's voice, loud and clear:

I have many enemies. And I will not have them know of your whereabouts.

He put on his coat and headed out with M'Baku.

T'Challa tapped his bus card against the reader, and M'Baku did the same.

"No forests to run through here," T'Challa said, once they'd found seats. He peered through the window. The Willis Tower loomed skyward, a blinking red light at the very top.

"We should go up there," M'Baku suggested. "I could spit, and we could see how far it goes."

"Yeah," T'Challa said in mock sincerity. "That would be completely fascinating."

The bus heaved its way down the street, stopping and starting with a lurch, and letting passengers off and on. T'Challa thought of home again. He needed to call his father.

"You know what Chicago has that we don't back home?" M'Baku asked, interrupting T'Challa's thoughts.

"What?"

M'Baku smiled, showing every one of his bright white teeth. "Pizza!"

Twenty minutes later, M'Baku wiped pizza grease from his lips and reached for another slice.

"That's your third, isn't it?" T'Challa asked.

M'Baku held up four fingers with his free hand.

The pizza place was called Antonio's, and they had picked it at random because there were so many to choose from.

T'Challa bit into his slice of pepperoni. "It's good," he said.

"Mmmmggg," grunted M'Baku.

T'Challa glanced around the restaurant. It felt strange to him. Most of the people were white, which was something he wasn't used to. Wakanda was an African country, and the people he grew up with were black. He was reminded of Hunter, and how he was looked at in Wakanda.

"Uh-oh," moaned M'Baku, his mouth full of pizza.

The door closed and three boys walked in.

It was Gemini Jones and his friends.

M'Baku slumped down in his seat a little. T'Challa did not.

"Let me get a slice of pepperoni," Gemini demanded from the man at the register. His two friends, Deshawn and Bicep, ordered something called "subs."

T'Challa swallowed his last bit of pizza right when Gemini turned around from the counter. Their eyes met. "Oh snap!" Gemini said. "It's Africa. Whatup, Africa?"

T'Challa didn't know what to say.

Gemini sauntered over, just like he had in the cafeteria. His friends tagged along behind him. He leaned in and rested his fingertips on the table. T'Challa noticed the ring again—a gleaming silver skull.

People are afraid of him because he says he's a warlock.

"Mind if we sit here?" Gemini said, and then slid in next to M'Baku, who barely had time to scrunch himself toward the window side of the booth. Deshawn scooted in next to Gemini, and Bicep sat next to T'Challa. The server brought their food and left quickly. T'Challa noticed that Deshawn and Bicep also sported skull rings.

"They got pizza in Africa?" Gemini asked, biting into his slice.

"No," said T'Challa.

Gemini chewed and nodded at the same time. Deshawn and Bicep said nothing, just stared at M'Baku and T'Challa like they were aliens from another planet. "In Chi Town, we do pizza all the time," Gemini boasted.

T'Challa didn't say anything. He was curious as to why Gemini and his friends decided to sit with them. It was a power play, he knew that much.

"You know," Gemini continued, and then wiped his mouth with the back of his hand, "I'm not that good with the fancy wrestling, but you know what I *am* good at?"

"No," T'Challa answered.

"*Arm* wrestling. Wanna go?"

"Go where?" T'Challa replied.

Gemini leaned back. He nodded his head a few times. "You're a funny dude, Africa. C'mon. Arm-wrestle me. Loser buys a whole pie."

M'Baku looked at T'Challa and raised an eyebrow. T'Challa picked up a napkin and wiped his hands. "All right, if you really want to."

"Uh-oh," Deshawn and Bicep both said, and then looked at each other with annoyed faces.

Napkins and plates were quickly moved. T'Challa rested his right elbow on the table. He and M'Baku used to arm-wrestle all the time when they were kids. Truth be told, T'Challa wasn't great at it, but Gemini's skinny arm didn't look too intimidating.

Gemini rubbed his hands together and then placed his elbow on the table. "Okay. Let's do this."

The boys clasped hands.

T'Challa stared at Gemini. He had the whisper of a little fuzz on his upper lip, and T'Challa imagined him standing in front of the mirror every morning trying to brush it.

"One," said Deshawn.

"Two," added Bicep.

There was a moment of silence. They turned to look at M'Baku.

"Three," he said.

Both boys leaned into the table. Gemini's grip was like a vise. The skull ring on his finger stood out and rubbed T'Challa's pinky finger.

"C'mon, Gemini," Deshawn encouraged him.

M'Baku looked at T'Challa. They didn't have to speak. M'Baku just gave him a curious tilt of the head, as if to say: *You gonna let this guy beat you?*

T'Challa breathed out and pushed himself further. His hand suddenly felt slick, and he didn't know if it was from the pizza grease or sweat. Both boys' elbows pivoted a little on the table.

Gemini was leaning in, and T'Challa felt the whole weight of his upper body trying to bend him to his will.

"Not bad, Africa," Gemini said, his voice straining.

My name's not Africa, T'Challa wanted to say. *It's T'Challa, Prince of Wakanda.*

Bang!

Gemini's knuckles hit the table.

T'Challa released his grip.

No one spoke.

Deshawn and Bicep looked at Gemini warily, waiting.

Gemini shook his wrist and flexed his fingers. "Took you long enough," he said lazily. "I could've gone longer, but got tired. Next time, bro."

He got up, and his friends rose with him, grabbing their half-eaten food. They seemed to follow his every lead.

"Hey," M'Baku called. "You owe us a pizza."

Gemini stopped midstep and turned around.

T'Challa grinned.

"I got your pizza right here," Gemini said, and made a rude gesture.

The door slammed shut, as Gemini and his friends left the pizza shop.

CHAPTER
ELEVEN

"I guess that's what you'd call a sore loser," M'Baku said a short time later.

The bus doors hissed open to let on more passengers.

"I know," said T'Challa. "Did you see the look on his face?"

M'Baku made a fake tough-guy face, scowling and tightening his lips.

"What's wrong with those guys?" T'Challa asked.

"I don't know," said M'Baku. "I think they're all bark and no bite."

"They all have the same ring. A silver skull. Did you see it?"

"Yup," M'Baku replied. "I guess all the warlocks wear them."

T'Challa grinned.

The bus made its way down Michigan Avenue. They weren't ready to go back to the embassy yet, so they decided to just ride for a while and take in some sights. Plus, they were both stuffed from pizza and needed a break.

T'Challa let his thoughts drift. He thought of Hunter, and how he and Gemini Jones were similar—always wanting to challenge people. Why? Maybe deep down inside they were both really insecure, and had to put on a show to appear tough. Whatever the reason, T'Challa thought it was a little sad.

He looked out the window. Beyond the wide sidewalk, crowds of people milled about in a park of some sort. One building stood out from the others and reminded him of home. Its surface was all steel or iron, with curved, polished sheets that created a fanciful design. "Let's check this out," he said.

"What?" asked M'Baku.

"Over there." T'Challa pointed. "In the park."

T'Challa pulled the cable for the next stop and then grinned at M'Baku, as if to prove he was city-smart.

They got off and crossed the street. The smell of roasting meat made T'Challa's mouth water, but his stomach was full.

"What's a gyro?" M'Baku asked, looking at the sign on

a parked truck. Other trucks were parked next to it, all selling food of some sort. Mingled aromas rose in the cold air.

"Don't know," T'Challa answered.

Sure enough, M'Baku just had to find out.

"Mmm," he moaned a minute later, angling his head to take another bite. Juice ran down his arms and onto his coat. "Tastes like chicken."

T'Challa turned and took in the sights around him. Street preachers, jugglers, drummers, and more all competed for space.

They headed toward the largest crowd. Several people were gathered around an object of some sort. They nudged their way through. T'Challa saw glints of metal, sparkling in the cold sunlight. "Interesting," he said.

A massive metal sculpture stood in front of them, its mirrored surface reflecting the people gathered around it.

"Is it an egg?" M'Baku asked.

"Some kind of bean," suggested T'Challa.

"They call it *Cloud Gate*," a voice spoke up.

T'Challa spun around.

He froze.

The man was familiar, even though he'd only seen him from a distance. It was the same man he saw that first day when they'd caught the bus to school. Now that he was closer, T'Challa noticed a scar on his cheek. Most curious of all was an eyepatch, placed over his left eye.

"But tourists call it the Bean," the man said.

T'Challa and M'Baku eyed each other.

"First time in Chicago?" the man asked.

"Uh, yeah," M'Baku answered.

There was a moment of silence, broken only by the chattering of tourists.

"C'mon, Marcus," T'Challa said. "We need to go. Remember?"

M'Baku took the hint, and both boys turned around and headed in the opposite direction.

"Who was that?" M'Baku asked, once they were a fair distance away.

"I don't know," T'Challa replied. "But I've seen him before. I think he may be following us."

The bus hit a pothole and both boys bounced in their seats. It was getting a little darker now, although it was only four in the afternoon. T'Challa looked out at Lake Michigan. Small waves crashed against massive rocks along the beachfront. Gray clouds moved across the sky, threatening rain. A small boat in the distance rocked unsteadily in the water, and T'Challa wondered why someone would be out there in such cold weather.

"Who do you think he is?" M'Baku asked again. "That man."

"I don't know," T'Challa replied. "That's why we need to be careful. He could be an enemy of my father's."

"Why do you think your father has so many enemies?"

It was a good question, T'Challa realized, and one he had never stopped to ask himself. "I suppose there are a lot of criminals out there that want to get at Wakanda's . . . you know."

"*Vibranium*," M'Baku whispered.

"Right. And maybe if they got to *me* they could get to him. For ransom, or something."

M'Baku nodded and leaned back in his seat.

"We need to stay close to the embassy," T'Challa said quietly. "We need to be *careful*."

"Yeah, yeah," M'Baku teased. "Gotta keep the mighty prince safe."

T'Challa shot him a look. He wasn't in the mood for M'Baku's joking taunts.

CHAPTER TWELVE

T'Challa took the exit stairwell and headed up the steps, away from M'Baku, who was asleep in their room after gorging himself on room service ice cream. There were nine floors in the embassy, and he was going to the very top. Hopefully, there would be a way onto the roof.

A few minutes later, he was standing in front of a green door in the dimly lit stairwell. He turned the handle: locked. A window to his left was closed by rusty hinges. He turned one of them, and the small red flakes fell away and onto the sill. He turned the other, and then slid the window up.

He stuck his head through. A cold blast of air greeted him and stung his cheeks. A fire-escape ladder on his right was positioned along the brick-and-steel wall. T'Challa let out a breath, reached across with his left arm, grasped the closest rung, and swung himself over to grab the other with his right. He then climbed up to the top of the roof.

He didn't have to go to such lengths, but something spurred him on. It felt a little dangerous. And, he had to admit, he missed those moments in Wakanda where he and M'Baku pushed themselves as far as they could.

The lights of Michigan Avenue glittered below him. He heard car horns and the hum of traffic. The night air was cool on his face. He tapped a bead on his Kiyomo Bracelet. A moment later, a screen appeared and hung in midair, his father's face projected upon it.

"Son," his father said.

"Father," said T'Challa. "How are you? How is the kingdom? Has there been any—"

"All is well at the moment," the king said. He rubbed his brow. "There was a small skirmish on the outskirts of the city, but we have driven the invaders back."

T'Challa was not convinced. His father's face was drawn. He looked tired.

"But how are *you*, T'Challa?" his father asked. "Are you and M'Baku staying safe?"

"Sure," he said. "But you know M'Baku. Always wanting to stir things up."

"Keep an eye on him. If anything happened to him, his father would never forgive me."

T'Challa thought that a little funny—his father being concerned with what one of his citizens thought of him. He was the king, and could do whatever he wished without consequence. But he still had a conscience. That was why people swore allegiance to him. He was a fair man, and a wise king.

There was something else T'Challa wanted to ask. He took a breath. "What about Hunter?"

The king drew back from the screen just a bit. He hesitated a moment before speaking. "I have given Hunter a very important position. Something that will help us keep the country safe."

T'Challa felt a stab of jealousy. "What is it?" he asked.

"I have started a security force. It is called the Hatut Zeraze."

"Dogs of War," T'Challa translated from Wakandan.

"You know Hunter is a great tracker, T'Challa. Even at his age. He's training young recruits in the art of stealth and maneuvers, just in case. . . ."

When the fighting starts, I'll be here by Father's side, not running off to hide in America.

T'Challa's face fell.

"Do not think of it as a slight, son," the king assured him. "Hunter is older, and he has a strong, if quick-to-act, mind. I can smooth that out. With time."

Say whatever you like, little brother. But while you're away, I'll keep your royal seat warm for you.

"T'Challa," the king said. "When you get back, you can work together. You and your brother, keeping Wakanda safe from invaders."

T'Challa feigned a smile. "Sure, Father. I will look forward to that."

There was a moment of silence. T'Challa couldn't think of what to say.

"How is the school?" his father finally asked. "How is Chicago?"

"It's okay," T'Challa replied, his thoughts still on Hunter.

"Good," his father said. He turned his head, leaving his face in profile on the screen. He nodded, as if someone was speaking to him. He turned his attention back to his son. "I must go, T'Challa. Take care of yourself, and if there is anything to report, I will be in touch."

And just like that, the screen winked out.

T'Challa looked out at the Chicago night. Hunter's face flashed through his mind. He saw him wearing a crisp uniform, complete with the Wakandan colors, and gaining his father's favor.

The Hatut Zeraze. A secret police force. *Why would Father give him such power?*

Hunter would surely try to boss him around when he got back to Wakanda.

I won't let him, T'Challa promised himself. *If he tries to order me around, he'll be in for a surprise.*

CHAPTER
THIRTEEN

T'Challa walked down the hallway, his thoughts still on Hunter and the conversation he had with his father. It had burned at him all night, and he still couldn't let it go. It was jealousy, plain and simple, but he didn't want to admit it.

He passed the spot in the hallway where the bundle of sticks had been placed. The buzz about it had died down, but it still stuck in his mind. There was something odd about it. Something *strange*. It was intentional, and was meant to make some kind of statement, but what that statement was, T'Challa didn't know. He almost tapped his Kiyomo Bracelet to set a reminder to look it up when he was alone, but suddenly remembered he couldn't do that here.

T'Challa entered the gym and breathed in the familiar aroma of dirty socks. The sound of balls hitting the hardwood floor was as loud as cannons. Above the noise, T'Challa heard several boys boasting:

I got mad skills!

You ain't got no game!

You play like your mama!

T'Challa definitely wasn't looking forward to P.E.

Today they'd be playing basketball, a sport T'Challa knew little about. M'Baku, on the other hand, was excited. In Wakanda, he had watched the Chicago Bulls play several times on old video files, and marveled at the players during the golden era of Michael Jordan and Scottie Pippen. A few other boys shared his passion, and they played often. T'Challa was not one of them. He was more interested in individual sports, like archery, climbing, and swimming—ones where the only person you had to beat was yourself.

T'Challa surveyed the scene around him. Gemini Jones, Deshawn, and Bicep were there in the crowd, flexing muscles and taunting other students, until Coach Blevins's whistle rang throughout the gym.

"All right," he called out. "Two teams. Red and white. Pick your own sides."

Everyone scrambled to a large cardboard box in the center of the gym. For a moment, T'Challa didn't know what was happening until several jerseys were pulled out. He walked over and picked up a white jersey from the floor. M'Baku chose red.

A few minutes later, after much pushing and shoving, which was only quieted by the intervention of Mr. Blevins, the teams were assembled. "Ah," M'Baku said, eyeing the jersey in T'Challa's hand. "Prepare to lose."

T'Challa smirked and pulled the white jersey over his T-shirt.

Gemini Jones and his friends were on M'Baku's team.

"Okay," Mr. Blevins said. "You all know the rules. No fouling and no elbows. Jump ball!"

The ball went up in the air and was retrieved by a tall boy on T'Challa's team. T'Challa didn't even know what position he was playing. Suddenly, the ball was flying in his direction. Someone had passed it to him. He threw out his arms in a reflex motion and caught it. It felt unfamiliar in his hands, like a large stone or a giant cake. He let it drop to the floor to dribble and . . .

Tweeeeeeeetttt!!!

Coach Blevins blew his whistle. "That's what we call a double dribble, Mr. Charles. And I'm pretty sure I caught a little traveling in there, too."

T'Challa didn't even know what he had done wrong.

The ball was passed in to M'Baku, who stood at the edge of the court. He bounced it a few times, walking, and then took off at a run. T'Challa was amazed. He seemed like he was born for it, a natural. He crossed the ball through his legs, spun away from an opposing player, then charged toward the net. He jumped and . . .

Swish.

Cheers went up from his teammates.

Coach Blevins nodded in approval. "Looks like we've got a new point guard." A few players clapped M'Baku on the back. Gemini Jones was one of them. "Not bad, Africa," he said.

M'Baku raised his hand for a high five, which Gemini returned.

Later that day, T'Challa sat in Study Hall and pondered a chess move. He tapped his finger on the carved wooden knight, one of his favorite pieces. He was distracted. After the basketball game in P.E., M'Baku had hung back with Gemini and his friends, laughing and joking. *What was that all about?* T'Challa wondered.

"Your move," Zeke said, moving his queen.

T'Challa immediately pounced and captured with his knight.

"What the—?" Zeke moaned, leaning in and staring at the board. "How'd you do that?"

"Like this," T'Challa said and made the move again.

Zeke shook his head. He brushed a hand through his close-cropped hair. "Want to play again?" he asked.

T'Challa checked his watch.

Zeke's brown eyes grew as wide as saucers. "Hey," he said. "Let me see that." T'Challa had been so concerned with not revealing the true nature of his Kiyomo Bracelet that he'd forgotten that his watch was even more unusual. It didn't look like an ordinary watch. It was a silver cuff about two inches wide, with an opaque black screen embedded into the surface.

T'Challa hesitated. He pushed up his sweater and thrust out his arm.

Zeke nudged his glasses up and stared at the device on T'Challa's wrist. "Where's the numbers?" he asked, perplexed. "I mean, I don't see anything."

T'Challa peered around the room. They were at a corner table, in the back. He laid the tip of his index finger against the glossy black surface. For a moment nothing happened, but then, the screen burst into color with swirling numerals and symbols. Zeke looked on in amazement as a small three-dimensional projection rose in the air, showing the time and date. The letters and numbers looked solid, as if they could be picked up. Zeke reached out a tentative hand.

T'Challa swiped his hand through the image, which then vanished.

Zeke's mouth hung open. "Where in the heck did you get that?"

T'Challa paused and looked around. Thankfully no one else had seen his little display of Wakandan tech. "I had it custom-made."

Zeke raised a skeptical eyebrow. "*Custom-made?* Where?"

T'Challa cursed himself. What was he thinking? "Back home," he said. "I had it made in Kenya."

"Hmpf," Zeke said. "Interesting."

T'Challa swallowed hard, and promised himself to be more careful in the future.

CHAPTER
FOURTEEN

T'Challa watched in fascination as his breath steamed in the air. It was cold out, but he and his friends wanted to get away from the noise in the cafeteria, so they sat outside on the bleachers that surrounded the football field. Zeke was reading one of his graphic novels, turning the pages silently, only pausing now and then to take a loud slurp through a straw, while Sheila sat nearby, fiddling with a small square cube of different colors.

"What's that?" T'Challa asked her.

"Some ancient toy," Zeke said, without looking up.

Sheila's hands moved quickly, almost in a blur. "Just

because you can't figure it out doesn't mean it's dumb," she replied.

T'Challa heard a resounding click. Sheila held up the small box. "It's called a Rubik's Cube."

"Can I see it?" T'Challa asked.

Sheila handed it to him.

T'Challa began to turn the sides of the square, clockwise and back.

"You have to get all the sides to match the same color," Sheila explained.

T'Challa cocked his head and went back at it.

"I could tell you the solution," Sheila taunted, "but that would take all the fun out of it."

T'Challa continued to turn and click the cube. "Ah," he said. "I see. . . ."

Loud shouting interrupted his concentration. He turned toward the outdoor basketball court. As cold as it was, a basketball game was being played, and Gemini Jones was dribbling the ball, playing aggressively and bumping into players. T'Challa watched M'Baku elbow his way through a player and slam the ball into the net.

"Nice!" Deshawn said.

Zeke looked up from his book. "Looks like Marcus found some new friends," he said quietly.

T'Challa was silent a moment. "Yeah," he finally said. "Looks that way."

"I'm not into basketball," Zeke said. "I mean, I don't *get* sports. Especially football. Why would people want to crash into each other like that?"

But T'Challa didn't really hear him. He was looking at M'Baku, who seemed to be having the time of his life.

Later that day, on the bus ride home, T'Challa nudged M'Baku. "So you're really into basketball, huh?"

M'Baku turned in his seat. "Yeah, the coach says I'd make a good point guard."

T'Challa nodded, even though he didn't know what a point guard was. "So, you like hanging out with Gemini and his friends?"

"They're okay once you get to know 'em. They get respect, you know?"

"Respect?"

"Yeah. I don't want people to think I'm just some exchange student from Africa. And since I can't tell anybody where I'm *really* from, I'm gonna make sure I get the respect I deserve."

T'Challa angled his head. This was just like M'Baku. Always concerned with what others thought of him. "So what are you gonna do?"

M'Baku shrugged. "I don't know. You can hang out with those nerds if you want to, but once I get on the team, I'm gonna change things up a little."

T'Challa narrowed his eyes. "What do you mean? What's wrong with Zeke and Sheila?"

"Gemini said they're losers. He said you need to hang out with the right people at South Side Middle."

T'Challa couldn't believe what he was hearing. The bus came to a stop and more passengers boarded. "So you're going to let other people tell you what to do?"

M'Baku didn't answer.

"Well," T'Challa finally said, breaking the silence, "Zeke and Sheila are okay in my book. It's not fair to call them nerds."

M'Baku gave a little smirk. "Whoever said life was fair, T'Challa?"

T'Challa opened his mouth in surprise but then closed it again. The bus hit a pothole and he bounced in his seat.

"See," M'Baku started, "you don't have to worry about stuff like that. You can get whatever you want, whenever you want. You're a *prince*, T'Challa. You were born with a silver spoon in your mouth. The rest of us have to earn it."

M'Baku turned away and looked out of the window.

They didn't speak for the rest of the way back.

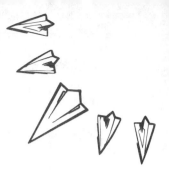

CHAPTER FIFTEEN

The posters were all over the school the next morning—in the cafeteria, the classrooms, even in the restrooms. There was no avoiding them:

SOUTH SIDE MIDDLE SCHOOL TALENT SHOW
Think you're a superstar?
Bring it!
Show us your best self and you could win
school supplies and movie passes!

Zeke and T'Challa stared at the yellow-and-green posters in the hallway. "What do you think?" Zeke asked. "Maybe we can have a chess tournament?"

"I don't think that'd be too exciting," T'Challa confessed.

"Well, maybe you could do a wrestling demonstration," Zeke suggested.

T'Challa thought about that. "I don't know," he said. "What about you? What other hobbies do you have?"

Zeke chewed his lip. "Well, I like to read a lot."

"I don't think that's going to work, either," T'Challa said.

"I know what I'm going to do." A voice sounded behind them. T'Challa turned around to see Sheila. She was carrying a small silver briefcase. "I'm going to do a science experiment."

"What kind of science experiment?" T'Challa asked.

"Well," said Sheila. "I'm going to make fog in the auditorium."

"Fog?" Zeke repeated. "How?"

"It's really not that difficult," Sheila said. "All I need are the right elements."

"Good luck with that," Zeke teased.

"Well, what's your special talent?" Sheila rounded on him. "Being a dork?"

"I know you are, but what am I?" Zeke shot back.

"I know *you* are," Sheila countered.

T'Challa whipped his head back and forth as they continued to chatter.

T'Challa had been so busy with things he had forgotten about his own science project. The teacher, Mr. Bellweather, had requested the assignment on his first day. He needed an idea. Fortunately, one came to him quickly.

Later that night, while M'Baku was practicing basketball, he approached the front desk to find Clarence, hunched over and typing. T'Challa coughed. Clarence looked up. T'Challa slid a piece of paper across the marble counter. "Do you know where I can get all this stuff?" he asked.

Twenty minutes later, after a short walk to a place called Walgreens, T'Challa looked at all the assembled parts spread out on the embassy room floor: a small motor, plastic wheels, metal rods, springs, nuts, bolts, assorted screws, and two small flashlights.

Wish I had some of my tools from Wakanda, he thought. *Oh, well, I'll just do something basic. Not too advanced.*

It took him an hour to build it.

He took it into Science class the next day, along with the TV remote from the embassy, which he had hacked.

"Who's next?" Mr. Bellweather asked. He was a tall man with a bald head and pants that were always too short. He looked at his tablet. "T. Charles, come on up."

T'Challa picked up the box from the floor and walked to the front of the classroom.

"So what did you make?" Mr. Bellweather asked.

"A robot," T'Challa answered.

Mr. Bellweather nodded, and T'Challa saw the disbelief behind his eyes. "Oh, really? Well, let's see, then."

T'Challa took the contraption out of the box and set it

on the floor. He pointed the remote at it and pressed PLAY. The little device whirred and clicked and then spun around. Everyone began to murmur and point.

Mr. Bellweather got up from his seat and looked at the small invention, turning and twisting. "I wanted to voice-activate it," T'Challa said, "but I didn't have time."

Mr. Bellweather walked in a circle around the robot, curious. "This is quite advanced, Mr. Charles. Where did you learn this?"

Advanced? T'Challa thought. He steered the robot out of a corner. "Just experimenting," he said.

A half hour later, T'Challa had a crowd around him in the lunchroom, as the robot turned in circles, blinked, and zoomed under tables and chairs.

Awesome!

Can you build me one?

Dude, your robot is sick.

"Sick?" T'Challa said. "What do you mean?"

Sheila laughed "That means *cool*, T."

Several people fell back as someone quickly pushed through the crowd.

A large brown boot came down on the robot.

CRUNCH!

Springs and screws went flying. The robot gave one last whir and then stopped moving.

T'Challa looked up.

It was Gemini Jones.

"Oops," Gemini said. "Sorry."

T'Challa's blood boiled. He took a step toward Gemini with clenched fists. Chairs scraped as people stepped back.

Uh-oh!

Fight!

"Break it up! Back in your seats!"

T'Challa turned around to see a teacher jogging over. She was tall, with her hair tied back in a severe ponytail. He thought she was the Girls' P.E. teacher. She looked down at the smashed robot. "Is this yours?" she asked T'Challa.

"It was," he said.

She turned to Gemini. "Should have known you'd be at the center of this, Mr. Jones. Did you do this?"

Gemini smirked. "Yeah, I broke his little robot. So what?"

The teacher tightened her lips. "My office," she said. "Now."

"Later, Africa," Gemini called as he followed the teacher away.

T'Challa looked down at his demolished creation. He bent to pick up the pieces.

He knew people like Gemini back in Wakanda. They usually came to no good end.

CHAPTER SIXTEEN

On the day of the talent show, kids filed into the auditorium, loud and boisterous. T'Challa sat with Zeke toward the front so they could get a good view of Sheila's presentation. A group of noisy boys way in the back made him turn around. M'Baku was sitting with a bunch of guys from Gemini's gang. He was pretty sure M'Baku saw him, but when their eyes met, his friend quickly turned away with a guilty expression.

T'Challa shook his head. Lately, he'd only seen M'Baku in the few classes they shared and at the embassy. He was spending a lot of time at basketball practice, and when he wasn't doing that, he was hanging out with Gemini Jones and his friends. He'd even given up sitting with T'Challa at lunch, and had joined Gemini and his pals at their table. T'Challa didn't want to admit it, but he was hurt.

He turned back around to see several students with musical instruments, including a tuba, saxophone, and bass drum. One girl was dressed in a ballerina outfit and another had a bow and arrow. *An archer?* T'Challa wondered. He hoped she was going to be safe. A whizzing arrow in the auditorium might not go over very well.

The buzzing in the auditorium grew louder. Right as it reached a fever pitch, Mrs. Evans walked onto the stage, her shoes clicking on the floor. "Welcome, everyone," she said, leaning into the microphone stand. "Quiet now. Calm down, please." The microphone squealed, and everyone covered their ears.

"Now," Mrs. Evans announced. "Our first contestant is Sheila Williams. So let's give her a warm South Side Middle School welcome!"

T'Challa and Zeke applauded and whistled loudly as Sheila came from behind the stage curtain. She carried a folding table that she set up quickly. She then opened her silver briefcase and placed several beakers on the table. Only then did she turn to the audience. The crowd burst into laughter.

Sheila wore safety goggles, which were a little too big

and made her eyes look huge. But Sheila ignored them and raised her head high. *Good for her*, T'Challa thought, and crossed his fingers.

Sheila took a deep breath. "Hello," she began, and her voice drifted out over the audience. "Today, I'm going to create fog in the auditorium."

Deafening silence.

Sheila coughed, and it created the loudest echo T'Challa had ever heard, bouncing off the walls and the high ceiling. She turned around and started fiddling with her lab instruments. T'Challa heard the clinking of a spoon against glass. He didn't know what she was doing, but she seemed completely focused. Finally, just as the audience was beginning to squirm a little, a cloud of purple mist rose up behind her. The whole crowd leaned forward. Mrs. Evans watched closely from the side of the stage.

The smoke rose, and instead of dissipating, another cloud of vapor appeared from Sheila's table.

There was a bang, and then a gasp. Mrs. Evans took a few steps forward. A cloud of purplish-red smoke rose up above Sheila, working its way to the ceiling. "Oooh," the crowd said in unison, craning their necks.

Sheila smiled, basking in the moment of admiration. She went back to her beakers, stirring, clinking, murmuring to herself. Another cloud of mist rose and joined the purplish-red smoke. It hung in the air like a stormcloud ready to burst. A storm of applause broke out as Sheila took a bow.

"Well," Mrs. Evans said, walking onto the stage after the fog had disappeared. "That was certainly spectacular, Sheila. Can you tell us how you did it?"

Sheila took off her safety glasses and rubbed her eyes. "Well, it's quite simple, really. It's a reaction between iodine and zinc. The exothermic reaction comes from the heat, although I may have used a little too much iodine."

Mrs. Evans smiled awkwardly. "Well," she said. "That was quite . . . interesting, Sheila. Let's give her another round of applause!"

The audience cheered and whistled. *She's great at science,* T'Challa thought, and wished he could share some of his Wakandan tech with her.

Sheila gave another bow, then packed up and left the stage.

"That was pretty awesome," Zeke said.

"Yup," T'Challa said. "Awesome."

T'Challa sat through a few more presentations, the most interesting being from a girl who sang what she called an "old medieval song." T'Challa wasn't familiar with it, but as her voice soared out over the auditorium, he was filled with a sense of peace.

But the mood was quickly broken.

Mrs. Evans walked out from the side of the stage. "Quiet now, everyone," she said. "We have one more demonstration." She looked at her notepad and cocked her head. "Mr. Gemini Jones?"

T'Challa felt just as befuddled as Mrs. Evans. What was he going to do? Arm-wrestle somebody?

"Robot killer," Zeke hissed.

Calls of *Yo! Gemini* went up in the crowd.

T'Challa watched Gemini saunter up to the stage. He took the microphone from Mrs. Evans and waved his other arm in the air, as the audience continued to applaud. Mrs. Evans wandered to the side of the stage again, looking a little bewildered.

Once everyone was settled, a hush fell over the auditorium. Gemini raised the microphone to his mouth. "I'm gonna need a volunteer," he said.

There was a little shuffling and murmuring and a girl stood up. "Aliyah!" someone in the crowd shouted.

T'Challa watched the girl named Aliyah take to the stage. She wore her hair in dreadlocks, which was also a custom in Wakanda.

"I need a chair," Gemini called. Mrs. Evans came back out with a small chair, which Aliyah sat on. She placed her palms on her knees. Mrs. Evans stood a few feet away.

Gemini turned to the audience. "Who believes in magic?" he asked.

A number of hands shot up into the air, including Aliyah's.

Gemini smiled. "Well, today you're gonna see something that's gonna blow your minds!"

Aliyah shifted in her seat. Mrs. Evans looked on curiously. Gemini turned to Aliyah, leaning down a little because he was so tall. He raised an open hand in front of her face. "What do you see on my palm?" he asked.

Aliyah leaned in, screwing up her face to get a closer look. "Nothing," she said.

The crowd laughed. "Some magic trick," someone called, to scattered chuckles.

Gemini looked to the audience and smiled. It was not a kind smile. He placed the microphone on the floor, stood up to his full height, and closed his eyes. He raised his hands to his mouth and cupped them, as if he were whispering words. After a moment, he dropped them. "Reveal," he said, and turned his palm toward Aliyah.

She screamed.

CHAPTER
SEVENTEEN

"But what did she see?" Sheila asked T'Challa.

"I don't know," he answered.

There were all kinds of rumors as to what Aliyah had seen. Some said it was a snake, others said it was a bug, and one person said it was her own reflection.

T'Challa was determined to find out what it was.

He didn't have the chance to ask her, though. Every time he saw Aliyah between classes she was surrounded by mobs of people. It looked to T'Challa like she just wanted to get away.

▲ ▲ ▲

Later that night at the embassy, T'Challa and M'Baku were both sprawled out on their beds. T'Challa was reading his science book while M'Baku flipped through a book about basketball. His mind kept drifting back to Gemini's strange feat of magic. "Do you know how Gemini Jones did that trick?" he finally asked.

"Nope," his friend replied, not taking his eyes away from his book.

T'Challa stiffened. M'Baku had become more and more distant these past few days. There was an awkward pause, something that had never happened between the two boys before.

"What's going on with you, M'Baku?" T'Challa demanded, finally breaking the silence that hung in the room. "You seem . . . I don't know. Different."

M'Baku placed his book on his outstretched knees. "Don't you ever get tired of staying here?" he replied, looking around the room as if it disgusted him. "I mean, we're in this huge city and we haven't really done anything. Gemini said I could stay with him and his dad if I wanted to. He said he'd show me around the city."

"What?" T'Challa said, surprised.

"He said they have great food every night and we can play video games as much as we want."

"We're supposed to keep a low profile," T'Challa reminded him. "Remember? Not wander around a strange city."

"I didn't come all the way over here to hide," M'Baku said.

T'Challa shook his head.

"Whatever," M'Baku replied.

The uncomfortable silence fell again. T'Challa went back to his homework. He really didn't understand what was going on with him.

M'Baku turned the pages of his book silently. It was like T'Challa wasn't even in the room with him. Finally, M'Baku looked up from his book. "Hey. I made the team. First match's tomorrow night. You coming?"

T'Challa let out a sigh. "Yeah," he said. "I'll be there."

The next day at school, T'Challa was on a mission. He put the trouble with M'Baku aside for a moment and made an effort to hunt down Aliyah and ask her what she had seen.

He found her between classes in the hallways as she was putting a book in her locker. This time she was alone. Her backpack had an image of a cat on it with a logo that read HELLO KITTY.

"Excuse me, Aliyah?" he asked quietly.

Aliyah turned around. She had kind green eyes and freckles, which T'Challa thought was quite unusual for someone dark-skinned. He liked her dreadlocks, too.

"Hi," Aliyah said. "You're T., right? You made that cool robot everybody was talking about."

"Yeah," he said, a little bashfully. *Until Gemini crushed it.*

They stood in silence for a brief moment as kids passed them in the hallway.

"Um," T'Challa started. "Well, I wanted to ask you a question."

Aliyah sighed. "About yesterday?"

Now T'Challa felt bad. He didn't want to bother her. He let out a breath. "I just—there are a lot of people saying stuff about what happened. If you don't mind"—he shuffled his feet—"can you tell me what you saw?"

Aliyah looked at the floor and then back up. She glanced left, and then right. "I only saw it for a second," she said.

"What?" asked T'Challa. "What did you see?"

Aliyah let out a big breath. "It was an eye," she whispered.

T'Challa stood motionless, not believing what he had just heard.

"I saw an eye," she said again. "An eye in the center of Gemini Jones's palm. It . . . winked at me."

CHAPTER EIGHTEEN

"What else do you know about Gemini Jones?"

The usual noise and activity in the lunchroom meant T'Challa had to raise his voice, but he looked around warily before asking.

"Why?" asked Sheila.

"I mean, do you think there's anything to this warlock business? Or does he just like to scare people?"

"I think it's true," Zeke said, looking up from his book. "One time Edwin Sharp said Gemini put a curse on him and he couldn't talk for a whole day."

"Couldn't talk?" T'Challa questioned.

Sheila looked up from her phone. "Oh, I remember

that. He said he couldn't move his mouth, right? Nobody believed him."

A moment of silence passed between them.

T'Challa shifted in his seat. "Aliyah said she saw an eye in Gemini's palm. She said it winked at her."

"Uh, that's weird," Zeke said.

"And," T'Challa continued, "Gemini and his friends all wear those skull rings."

"They're probably just trying to be creepy," Zeke suggested.

"Maybe," T'Challa said.

A scream rang through the cafeteria.

Heads swiveled.

"What the—?" Zeke said, standing up.

Squeaking chairs and raised voices filled the lunchroom. A crowd was forming, huddling in a corner by the exit. T'Challa and his friends rushed to the commotion. T'Challa pushed his way to the front.

His breath caught in his throat.

There it was again.

Another one of those weird stick things, like the one he had seen his first week at school.

But this one was different.

There was blood around it.

T'Challa looked left, then right. Everyone was focused on the strange object at their feet. He quickly pushed up his sleeve and pressed a small bead on his Kiyomo Bracelet.

▲ ▲ ▲

T'Challa ducked into an empty room before he went to his French class. He closed the door and tapped a bead on his bracelet. A small screen appeared in midair, projecting an image of the mysterious object he had just seen in the lunchroom. He looked to the door with apprehension and then tapped the screen. Small lines of code began running along the bottom of the image, ending in a beep. T'Challa looked at the result:

Devil's Trap
American Voodoo/Hoodoo
Used to capture or summon spirits and demons

T'Challa tapped the bead and the image flashed out. He had heard of Voodoo. It was an old religion, and several groups in Wakanda practiced it. They had their own ways, they said, and didn't believe in the Panther God, Bast, or in following the king's rules. T'Challa's father let them be, as long as they didn't try to influence others.

Now he was really curious. Did Gemini have something to do with this?

"It's called a Devil's Trap," T'Challa told Zeke and Sheila later that day. "I looked it up."

"Devil's Trap," Zeke said flatly. It wasn't a question.

"What are they for?" Sheila asked.

"It's some kind of Voodoo," T'Challa said. "For capturing spirits." He paused. "Or . . . summoning them."

Zeke swallowed. "Why would somebody put one here? In the school?"

"Somebody's playing jokes," Sheila said. "Halloween's coming up. Remember?"

T'Challa wasn't so sure about that.

Something was going on at South Side Middle School.

And he was going to find out what it was.

CHAPTER NINETEEN

"Wildcats! Wildcats! *Gooooo* Wildcats!"

The cheerleaders' chants combined with the rattle of snare drums soared out over the audience. T'Challa sat in the bleachers with Zeke and Sheila. The noise was deafening, but it didn't drown out his thoughts about the strange Devil's Trap or Gemini's trick.

"I don't know why you dragged me to this," Zeke complained.

"Well," Sheila said, "I *like* basketball. Wildcat spirit, you know?"

Zeke shrugged.

"Thanks for coming," T'Challa said. "Both of you. I didn't want to come by myself."

"You owe me," Zeke said, and then took a book out of his backpack.

Tweeeetttt!

The game started to thunderous applause. The Razors, an opposing team from a school downstate, took to the court in a frenzy. T'Challa spotted M'Baku in the Wildcats lineup.

T'Challa followed the game with interest, and he definitely saw the skill involved. It seemed that M'Baku was at the center of every big play, from three-point shots to stealing the ball. At halftime, T'Challa watched in fascination as a student in a Wildcat costume jumped around like a maniac.

"Is it over yet?" Zeke asked, looking up from his book.

"This is the last period," Sheila told him. "Score is tied."

"Fascinating," Zeke replied, and then went back to his book.

T'Challa watched the dynamics between M'Baku and Gemini Jones. They were on the same wavelength when it came to playing, and seemed to anticipate each other's thoughts. The play flowed seamlessly between them. T'Challa felt a twinge of resentment.

Was he jealous? Was that what this was all about?

No, he told himself. He just didn't *like* Gemini Jones— didn't like the way he approached him when they first met, didn't like the way he demanded to arm-wrestle, and definitely didn't like the way he destroyed his robot.

"Uh-oh," Sheila said. "Just a minute left."

The crowd in the gym leaned forward on the bleachers. T'Challa looked up at the scoreboard: Wildcats 98, Razors 99.

"Only ten seconds left!" Sheila exclaimed.

The roar rose to a fever pitch. A chant of "Wildcats! Wildcats!" rang in T'Challa's ears. Drumming feet on the bleachers shook the whole gym.

The ball was passed to M'Baku. T'Challa felt his heart in his chest. It *was* exciting.

M'Baku drove down the court. He spun, just like that time in gym class. He shot and—

Swish!

—scored the winning point.

Students rushed onto the court screaming and shouting. The team was mobbed. M'Baku pumped his fist in the air. Sweat rolled off him in waves. A group of players lifted him up. "Marcus! Marcus!" they chanted as they paraded him around the court. "Marcus! Marcus!" M'Baku's smile was brighter than T'Challa had ever seen it. He was basking in the moment, the center of attention, just like he always wanted. The opposing players took to the sidelines, defeated.

"Wow," Sheila said. "That was some game."

"Yeah," T'Challa said. "It was."

T'Challa, Sheila, and Zeke stepped down from the bleachers. The Wildcats trooped through on their way to the lockers, receiving high fives and congratulations from students and teachers alike. T'Challa spotted M'Baku and took a deep breath. "That was a good game," he said. "Nice shot at the end there."

"Thanks, man," M'Baku replied. "I was just like Michael Jordan!"

"Yo, Marcus." Gemini Jones jogged up behind M'Baku and clapped him on the shoulder. "We're all going for pizza. Coach's treat." He finally looked at T'Challa. "Team only."

T'Challa smirked.

M'Baku nodded. "Catch ya later, T.," he said, and continued on to the lockers.

Gemini glanced back at T'Challa when he and M'Baku were a few steps away. "Yeah," he piped sarcastically, "later, T."

T'Challa stood on the sidelines and watched his friend disappear into the crush of players and fans.

CHAPTER
TWENTY

T'Challa and his friends filed out of the gym and headed for the exit. A blast of cold air greeted him as Zeke opened the door. They stood in the parking lot and watched teachers and parents get into cars to head home. The black asphalt glittered under the tall lampposts spread throughout the lot.

"It's still early," Sheila said. "I'm hungry. Anybody up for pizza?"

A short walk later, they found a pizza shop in Hyde Park, one of the South Side's bigger neighborhoods. T'Challa ordered a slice of deep-dish topped with peppers, mushrooms, and pepperoni. Sheila had a garden salad while

Zeke ate a cheesesteak. T'Challa bit into his slice. *If M'Baku can go out with his new friends,* he thought, *so can I.*

"I was thinking," Sheila started. "Those things in the school. Those Devil's Traps."

T'Challa swallowed. "What about them?"

"It's just all so weird," Sheila said. "The traps, Gemini's trick."

"Maybe they're connected," Zeke said. "It'd be just like him to summon a demon."

"One problem," Sheila said.

"What?" Zeke asked.

Sheila speared a cherry tomato with her fork. "Demons aren't real."

T'Challa's thoughts drifted as he took the bus home. Maybe Gemini *was* some sort of warlock, and he was using a spell to lure M'Baku away. But to what purpose?

T'Challa got off the bus a block early and walked back to the embassy. The cold wind stung the tips of his ears. He passed a shop with sports gear in the window. Life-like mannequins stood frozen in their basketball jerseys and baseball caps.

A dark shadow ahead of him slipped into an alley.

T'Challa thought he caught a glimpse of a beret—or was he just seeing things? Was it the man again? The one he was sure was following him?

He took a few short steps and stood at the mouth of the alley.

There was no one there, just the silhouette of a rat, scrabbling between piles of trash.

T'Challa slid his key card through the embassy room door and stepped inside.

M'Baku looked up from an open suitcase, stuffed with clothes.

T'Challa stood there, mouth hanging open. "M'Baku, what are you doing?"

M'Baku threw a basketball jersey into the suitcase. "I'm gonna stay with Gemini and his dad for a while. I need to get out of here. See more of the city."

T'Challa walked in and closed the door behind him. He sat down on his bed. "Do you really think that's smart? If your father found—"

"But he won't, will he?" M'Baku cut him off. "Unless someone happens to tell him."

T'Challa sighed. What could he do? He couldn't force him to stay, and if he told his father, M'Baku would get in even *more* trouble.

"M'Baku," he started. "Look, I know you want—"

"I'm tired of living in your shadow, T'Challa."

The words struck T'Challa like arrows.

M'Baku moved the clothes around in his suitcase without really organizing anything. "Ever since we were little,

I've always been second fiddle." He raised his arms in a grand gesture. "Friend to the mighty prince. Well, it's time I made my own way, and I'm gonna do it *here*. In Chicago."

T'Challa was stunned. He shook his head. "What do you mean?"

M'Baku shrugged. "I don't know." He zipped up the suitcase and pulled it off the bed. "Maybe I'll stay here instead of going back to Wakanda. Gemini said his dad could help me out for a while. Maybe I'll get a basketball scholarship, you know? Join the pros."

"I don't think it's that easy," T'Challa said.

"See," M'Baku said with a grim smile. "There you go. Thinking I'm not as good as you."

"I didn't mean it like—"

"Whatever," M'Baku said, grabbing his jacket.

"What's Gemini up to?" T'Challa asked quickly, before the chance was gone. "Those skull rings? What's that all about? Do you know anything about those weird nest things?"

M'Baku pulled up the handle of his suitcase with a click. "No," he said, and made his way to the door.

"M'Baku, don't," T'Challa urged him.

But M'Baku opened the door, and, without looking back, wheeled his suitcase out.

CHAPTER
TWENTY-ONE

The glow from the Chicago skyline peeked through the closed curtains. T'Challa lay in bed, thinking.

It felt weird without M'Baku in the room.

Why would his friend just up and leave?

I should call Father, he thought. *Tell him what's going on. No. I need to figure this out on my own.*

Whatever's going on with M'Baku is between the two of us.

The next school day passed quickly, but T'Challa was distracted. He was thinking of M'Baku, Gemini, and the Devil's Trap. What were they really for? His search said that they were used to capture spirits—or summon them.

Were there spirits or demons in the school? Or was there some other purpose to them?

All of these thoughts swirled around in his brain until the last bell rang and he met up with his friends. "I have to tell you something," T'Challa started, as they made their way to the bus. "It's about Marcus."

Sheila and Zeke looked at him with curious faces.

"What did he do?" Zeke asked.

T'Challa hesitated. "He, um, left the host family we've been staying with. He didn't get along with them, so he said he's going to stay with Gemini Jones and his dad."

"What?" Sheila said. "That's nuts."

"I know," T'Challa agreed. "Gemini's been influencing him somehow. Ever since they started playing basketball together, he's changed. I know Gemini's up to something. I can feel it."

"Maybe he really *is* a warlock," Zeke said.

A moment of silence fell. Sheila narrowed her eyes, considering.

T'Challa paused. *Is that possible?*

There were plenty of Wakandan ghost stories and tales of terrible monsters, but they were all just imaginary. Weren't they?

"You know the woods behind the school?" Zeke asked.

"Yeah," Sheila replied.

"Well, every Wednesday, I see Gemini, Deshawn, Bicep, and some other people headed back that way."

"Maybe they've got some kind of secret club that meets back there," said T'Challa.

"Only one way to find out," Sheila added.

That night, before meeting up with Zeke and Sheila, T'Challa sat on the bed in his room. He ran his hand through his hair. He looked at his watch.

I need to tell Father about M'Baku.

Wait, another voice in his head advised him. *Give M'Baku a little time. He'll come to his senses.*

But he really wasn't sure about that at all.

He got up and walked to the safe. He wanted to see his suit for some reason, a reminder of home. The Panther suit was in there, along with the ring. He opened the safe and slipped the ring on his finger. *I shouldn't wear it,* he thought, and placed it back in the box. He ran his fingers along the silky black suit. He grasped it between his hands and pulled as hard as he could. The fabric stretched but did not tear or offer any resistance. *Well,* he thought, *I can at least try it on.*

It only took him a minute to get out of his school clothes and slip into the suit. An unfamiliar figure stared back at him through the mirror.

He was in form-fitting black, and shadows rippled along the fabric when he moved. There was a weave in the cloth he hadn't noticed before, like a small honeycomb mesh pattern. The mask covered his eyes.

His father's suit was equipped with boots, but T'Challa didn't have those. He also didn't have the ceremonial claw necklace to wear around his neck. But still, he looked pretty intimidating. His father said the suit was infused with Vibranium, the energy-absorbing material that was so highly valued around the world. T'Challa spun on his foot and struck a pose, his hands clenched into fists. His body felt lighter. Quicker. He jumped.

Crash!

He uncrumpled himself from the floor.

He had hit the ceiling.

It was the kinetic energy—absorbing and bouncing back.

He rubbed his head and decided to put the suit back into its box.

For now, he thought.

At 7:00 p.m., T'Challa slipped out of the embassy to meet up with Zeke and Sheila. A dark forest loomed behind the chain-link fence that bordered the football field.

"Remind me why we're doing this in the dark again?" Sheila asked.

"Because it's a secret mission," Zeke replied, slinging off his backpack. "We don't want to be seen."

T'Challa thought of his suit again and wondered if he should have put it on. But he was only going into the woods, he reminded himself. His father said not to wear it unless it was an emergency. This wasn't an emergency, just curiosity that had gotten the better of him. And he surely couldn't wear it in front of Zeke and Sheila.

Zeke reached into his backpack and took out a flashlight, then turned on the switch. There was no light.

"Great," Sheila said.

Zeke tapped the flashlight against his palm a few times until the light flickered and remained steady. "Okay," he said. "Let's do it."

"Are you sure about this?" T'Challa asked Zeke.

"I may be a geek," Zeke replied, "but no one ever said I was a scaredy-cat."

Sheila smiled. "Me too," she said, looking into the woods.

Zeke tapped the flashlight, which had gone out again.

"You know they have phones that have flashlights now," Sheila said. "You know. Smartphones?"

"I'm old-school," Zeke said. "Plus, who ever had a secret mission in the dark without a flashlight?"

T'Challa wrapped his coat around him a little more snugly as he walked. It was cold, and his toes felt numb in his boots. Zeke shone the flashlight along the ground, but there was enough moonlight to see by. Crickets and little night creatures stirred in the underbrush. It didn't bother T'Challa. He was used to wildlife and the forest, having grown up in a place that praised nature and the wild things in the world.

He was reminded of the exploring he and M'Baku used to do when they were little.

T'Challa looked up at the moon, obscured by fast-moving clouds. Perhaps his father was looking at that same moon now, back home in Wakanda. The memory made him recall the walks they took together, and how he learned of his grandfather, King Azzuri the Wise. He had listened with wide eyes as his father told him fantastical stories of Captain America and Sgt. Fury and his Howling Commandos. Maybe, T'Challa thought, he'd meet some of those great heroes one day.

They stepped out of the denser woods into an open area. A broken-down house stood in front of them. It looked to T'Challa like the whole thing could collapse at any minute. The shutters were splintered and hanging off, the remains of a crumbled chimney had caved in, and the windows were shattered.

"Why would someone build a house in the middle of the woods?" Sheila asked.

"More like a hunter's cabin or something," Zeke said.

"But we're still in the city," said Sheila. "You probably can't hunt in the city limits."

T'Challa took in his surroundings. Blackened tree branches and burnt tin cans were littered all around. "Whatever the reason," he said quietly, "it looks like it's been abandoned for years."

"What a dump," Zeke said.

"C'mon," T'Challa said. "I want to see what's inside."

Zeke and Sheila both swallowed at the same time.

T'Challa led the way as they entered through the space where a door once stood. Old furniture, fast-food wrappers, and newspapers littered the floor. T'Challa thought he saw a mouse scuttling in the heaps of trash.

They walked quietly, and Zeke kept the flashlight pointed at the ground in front of them. Rooms were on either side, some with doors and some without. As they passed one room, Zeke flashed the light and T'Challa saw discarded furniture, several boxes of trash, and a bunch of car parts scattered on a tarp on the floor.

T'Challa suddenly paused. He held up a fist. Zeke and Sheila froze behind him. "You hear that?" he whispered.

"Hear what?" Sheila asked.

T'Challa looked from left to right. "Voices," he said, and then pointed a finger straight ahead, where the darkness seemed to fade into light, just by a few degrees. "C'mon," he said. "*Quietly.*"

T'Challa felt a sense of dread as they began to walk again. The house wasn't *right*. It felt bad to him, as if something terrible had happened here. Or, he thought, was about to. Right before they reached the end of the hall, T'Challa brought them to a halt.

"*Now* I hear the voices," Zeke said.

"Me too," Sheila added.

T'Challa followed the muffled sound. "In this room," he whispered.

The three of them stepped quietly inside a room to their right. Broken pieces of lumber were under their feet. The one window in the room let in moonlight, which spilled along the ruined floor. "Turn off the flashlight!" T'Challa whisper-shouted.

Zeke immediately turned it off.

Darkness.

T'Challa knelt and put an eye up to one of the many broken patches in the wall. Zeke and Sheila did the same.

T'Challa gasped.

In the room ahead of him, through the broken slat of wood, several small figures formed a circle around a tree stump set with candles. They were kids, T'Challa realized. They had to be. They were all blindfolded. Orange flames flickered in the dark.

"What the—?" Zeke started.

"Shh!" Sheila said through closed teeth.

The kids stood like sheep herded into a pen. Several others wearing all black surrounded them. Three Devil's Traps were placed on the floor, forming a triangle. A shadowy figure emerged from a deeper shade of black.

T'Challa knew that silhouette. It was taller than anyone else.

Gemini Jones.

He took a walk around the group, displaying that same

cocky arrogance T'Challa had seen before. Finally, he paused and took a deep breath. "To become part of our order," he began, "you must swear your life to the Skulls."

"*Skulls*," T'Challa whispered.

Gemini lifted his chin, and one of the other boys in black—he thought it was Bicep—picked up a bag from the ground. He brought it to Gemini, who pulled a drawstring to open it. He reached inside—

—and took out out a gleaming human skull.

"Gross," Zeke whispered.

Sheila nudged Zeke in the ribs.

Gemini held up the skull with one hand and turned in a circle, as if addressing the whole world—the whole universe, even. "This is the skull of my great-grandfather, Thaddeus Jones," he announced, "the first Grand Mage of the Ancient Order of the Skulls."

T'Challa couldn't believe what he was hearing.

"He was powerful," Gemini continued. "He knew that to rise up in this world, you had to be feared. That is true power." He paused. "Now kiss the skull, and be one with our order."

T'Challa's stomach turned. The blindfolded kids murmured and shifted where they stood.

"The longer you wait," Gemini warned them, "the less power you will receive."

One by one, the blindfolded were pushed forward, while Gemini lowered the skull to be kissed.

T'Challa swallowed hard.

"Now you must swear," Gemini said. "Raise your left hands."

Hands went up in the air.

"Repeat after me," Gemini said. "'I swear my life to the Skulls . . . in this life and the next.'"

T'Challa shuddered as a chorus repeated the words back.

"'I swear to this oath, and may I be turned to ash if I do not abide.'"

"Jeez," Sheila whispered, hovering behind Zeke.

There was a moment of silence after the last words were repeated.

"Now," Gemini finally said, once more taking a walk around the group. "You may think that you have now passed into our order. But you are mistaken."

T'Challa saw one of the candidates turn left, then right, as if afraid, and wanting to run. One of the leaders grasped him by the arms.

"You're not going anywhere," Gemini commanded. "You still have to swear on the Book."

Gemini placed the skull on the tree stump, and then reached back into the bag. T'Challa closed one eye to focus. Gemini drew out a large book with a tattered cover.

He opened it.

And then he began to chant.

As the words left his lips, T'Challa felt a sense of unease. It was a language that was unfamiliar, yet he felt as if he had heard it somewhere before. Gemini paused in front of each candidate as he spoke, and they repeated the words back, while laying their hands upon the book. Sometimes Gemini had to correct them as they stumbled.

Finally it was over. Moonlight shone down into the room from a hole in the ceiling, as if it had been timed that way.

"Now," Gemini Jones said, and he held his head high, "rise . . . rise as a member of the Ancient Order of the Skulls!"

Deshawn removed the blindfolds. Several girls were among the newly initiated.

"Equal-opportunity creep," Sheila quipped.

But T'Challa had gone still.

The last one to have their blindfold removed was a face he knew well.

M'Baku's.

CHAPTER
TWENTY-TWO

The return bus trip home was quiet. The three of them barely spoke. T'Challa's thoughts were scattered: blindfolded kids, Gemini and his skull, M'Baku. . . .

"Well," Sheila said. "At least we know why they're called the Skulls."

"Why?" T'Challa asked.

"Because they're all a bunch of boneheads," Sheila snapped.

"There's a secret society right in our school," Zeke said in amazement. "It's like something from one of my books."

"But it's real," Sheila said.

"They had a skull," Zeke said. "A human skull!"

T'Challa didn't need to be reminded.

"This is us," Zeke said, as he and Sheila rose from their seats. "See you tomorrow."

"Right," T'Challa said absently. "Tomorrow."

"Hey," Zeke called before he got off. "You never said where you live."

T'Challa swallowed. "I'm a bit farther up."

Zeke nodded. "Oh, well, if you take the—"

Sheila closed her eyes and opened them again slowly. "You're worried about bus routes? After what we just saw?"

Zeke shrugged.

T'Challa was glad Sheila interrupted him, because he didn't have a quick answer ready.

T'Challa slipped back into the embassy unnoticed, and opened the door to his room. He tapped a communication bead on his Kiyomo Bracelet immediately. "Ancient Order of the Skulls," he said. A screen rose up around him. After a moment, there was a beep and small lines of text appeared.

Skulls, rumored to be an American secret society. Founded 1930s. No known facts or information. Said to be founded by Thaddeus Jones (deceased), once described as an African American mystic and occultist.

Gemini's words came back to him.

This is the skull of my great-grandfather, Thaddeus Jones. The first Grand Mage of the Ancient Order of the Skulls.

He knew a little about secret societies. In Wakanda, there were several, and they were always jockeying for power. His father called them usurpers, people who wanted to take his throne and sell vast amounts of Vibranium for their own personal reward.

T'Challa slipped out of his coat and sat down in a chair. What was his friend doing in that crazy ritual? M'Baku's father had taught him better than that. He just didn't understand.

T'Challa slept fitfully and awoke several times during the night. He kept seeing Gemini Jones in that dark room, slowly turning in a circle, the ghastly skull held up to the moonlight coming through the roof.

This is the skull of my great-grandfather, Thaddeus Jones.

And what about the words he spoke? What did they mean? And the book the kids swore upon?

At some point, he must have fallen asleep, because the next thing he knew . . .

BEEP . . . BEEP . . . BEEP . . .

T'Challa reached out from under the covers and shut off the alarm. He looked across the room and thought he might see M'Baku, but no such luck. He was gone. And then it all came rushing back. . . .

The Ancient Order of the Skulls
Candles on a tree stump
A gleaming human skull
M'Baku

He pushed the weird thoughts to the back of his mind and got ready for school.

Sheila found him at lunchtime and cornered him, her eyes wide. "You're not going to believe this," she said breathlessly.

Five minutes later, T'Challa, Sheila, and Zeke were in the cafeteria. The noise and clatter of activity set T'Challa's nerves on edge.

"What is it?" T'Challa asked.

Sheila flipped open her tablet. "Remember the words Gemini was speaking last night? The ones we didn't understand?"

"Yes," T'Challa and Zeke said at the same time.

"It was Old Nubian," Sheila said proudly.

"Old what?" Zeke asked.

And that's when T'Challa remembered.

"What?" Sheila asked. "What is it?"

T'Challa paused. "Some of the words. They seemed familiar. Like I've heard them back home."

"Maybe it's from the same family of languages," Sheila suggested. "Old Nubian is *ancient*. It's one of the oldest

African languages, going all the way back to the fourth century."

T'Challa felt a twinge of envy. *He* should have been the one to recognize the language first. "Wait," he started. "How did you—?"

Sheila waggled her cell phone in front of him. "I had it on audio record."

"Excellent move," said Zeke.

"All I had to do was transcribe it," she said "Look." She flipped the tablet around so T'Challa and Zeke could see the screen. T'Challa mouthed the words in front of him:

Darkness falls,
And He shall awaken.
Swear to Him,
And ye shall be rewarded.

A cold chill crept up T'Challa's neck. He swallowed. "What in the world is this?"

"Some kind of spell," Zeke said, a tremor in his voice.

"Spell?" Sheila shot back. "There's no such thing as spells. This isn't the Dark Ages."

T'Challa leaned back from the table. He knew this wasn't true. In Africa and Wakanda the old magic was still practiced, and there were many people who fell victim to curses and dark spells. Or, at least, they claimed they had.

"Who is 'He'?" Zeke asked. "Swear to who?"

"'Whom,'" Sheila corrected him.

"Whatever," Zeke said.

The sunlight in the cafeteria disappeared, blotted out by dark clouds. The three students sat very still for what seemed like minutes. The noise around them slowly morphed into one constant hum, one that seemed to pierce T'Challa's ears.

His father had told him tales of monsters, demons, and spirits when he was a child, but those were just fireside tales, weren't they? Did those things really exist in the modern world?

Darkness falls,
And He shall awaken.

What did it mean?

He didn't have an answer, but he knew he had to find out.

CHAPTER
TWENTY-THREE

The school day was done, and T'Challa and Zeke were just finishing up a chess match. Truth be told, T'Challa hadn't been able to concentrate at all. He'd made his moves without careful thinking, something Zeke had caught on to and taken advantage of.

There was something he had to do. There was no way around it.

T'Challa drummed his fingers on the table and let out a sigh. "Zeke?"

"Yeah?"

"Do you know where Gemini Jones lives?"

Zeke tilted his head. "Why do you want to know that?"

"Marcus said he was staying with him. Remember?"

Zeke paused a moment before speaking. "So, let me get this straight. Marcus not only joined the Skulls, now he's living with their leader? Why would he—"

"I don't know," T'Challa interrupted. "Like I said before, he's had problems with his host family. You know. Since we've been here."

Zeke nodded slowly, like he wasn't sure he should believe T'Challa's explanation. "Hey," he said, fiddling with a pawn on the board and not meeting T'Challa's gaze. "You never said where *you* live. When I asked you last night. Where do you stay, anyway?"

T'Challa stiffened. His brain ran in circles. *Think.* "One of my uncles has a place on Michigan Avenue," he blurted out. *Another lie,* he thought with regret. He was amazed at how quickly he could deceive people.

"Ah," Zeke said, and then, after a brief pause: "Wait a minute. The other day you said 'the host family *we've* been staying with.' You and Marcus. So which is it? Are you staying with your uncle or a host—?"

"Zeke!" T'Challa bristled. "Where does Gemini Jones live?"

Zeke shrank in his seat.

T'Challa immediately regretted his outburst. "I'm sorry," he said. "I'm just worried about my friend."

Zeke let out a breath. "I know," he said contritely,

pushing up his glasses. "I would be too, if my friend went around kissing a dead man's skull."

T'Challa swallowed.

"He lives over by the big Greek church on Wentworth and Twenty-Ninth Street. You can't miss it. It's got a sculpture in the front yard. Kind of like a big animal thing."

T'Challa nodded and made a mental note. "Okay," he said. "Thanks. I'll see you soon, Zeke. And sorry."

"No problem," Zeke answered.

T'Challa turned to leave.

"Hey, T.," Zeke called.

T'Challa turned around.

"Be careful."

T'Challa smiled. "I will," he said. "I know how to take care of myself."

Zeke nodded, but the half smile he returned was a troubled one.

T'Challa walked with his hands stuffed in his pockets and braced himself against the wind that came swirling off the lakefront. He really shouldn't have blown up at Zeke, he realized. He was just asking questions, something any friend would have done. *I have to start being more careful. Patient. That's what Father would say.* Nothing was ever accomplished through anger. T'Challa promised himself he would take his father's wise advice.

He had to try talking to M'Baku once more—make him

come to his senses. They'd been friends since childhood, and T'Challa wasn't going to give up on him that easily.

He thought of taking a bus, but wasn't sure how often they ran. He passed basketball courts and check-cashing shops, liquor stores, and churches. As he turned onto Wentworth, a group of boys in big coats came sauntering in his direction. Zeke had told him to be careful, but T'Challa wasn't afraid. He was a prince, after all, and could certainly handle himself.

The sidewalk was only so big, and the boys didn't look like they were going to move, so T'Challa stepped aside, but not before one of them bumped into his shoulder.

"Watch where you're going, man," one of them said.

T'Challa paused but did not speak. The boy drew a little closer. He had at least three inches' height on T'Challa.

"You owe me an apology," the boy said. The other boys grouped in a circle around T'Challa, as if he were an antelope being sized up by lions, something he had seen more than once.

"You heard the man," one of them said. "Apologize, son."

T'Challa looked from left to right, keeping an eye on their movements. "I'm not your son," he said. *I am the son of T'Chaka,* he wanted to say. *The Black Panther and King of Wakanda.*

The boy cocked his head. "What's wrong, dude? You can't hear?" He brushed imaginary debris from his shoulder. "You bumped into me. Got dirt on my coat. Apologize."

Someone grabbed T'Challa's throat from behind.

T'Challa drove his right elbow back into his attacker's stomach, then spun around quickly and struck the boy in the chest with the heel of his left palm. The boy doubled over and flew back.

Another kid lunged.

T'Challa caught his arm and struck down hard at his elbow.

Snap.

The remaining boy bounced on his toes and held up both fists, but dropped them after a fiery glare from T'Challa.

"It's cool, man," the boy said, raising his hands in defeat and slowly stepping back. "No worries, bro."

And then he took off running, leaving both of his friends on the ground, rolling around in pain.

T'Challa looked at his attackers for a long moment. "I'm sorry," he finally said. "But I'm really not your son." He shook his head and turned, then quickly made his way down the street.

T'Challa looked back and saw the two boys pick themselves up from the ground. They seemed to be arguing with each other, raising their arms and shouting. He squared his shoulders and continued on, glancing behind him every now and then, just to make sure they weren't regrouping for another attack.

I didn't want to hurt them, he thought, his heart still racing. *But I have to protect myself. That's what Father's always said.*

After another minute or two, T'Challa passed a massive church with stained-glass windows and onion-shaped domes on the very top. Rows of houses were on the opposite side of the street. One was set apart from the others, on its own lot. There was no mistaking it. The whole house was surrounded by a high fence, except for a gate at the entrance, set far from the walkway. A metal sculpture that seemed to be made from rusted car parts sat in the front yard. It reminded T'Challa of a griffin—a mythological creature with the body of a lion and the wings of an eagle. Sharp metallic talons gripped the block of wood it perched upon.

Strange, he thought.

He unlatched the gate and walked down a flagstone path, which led to a row of little white steps. He rang the buzzer. He heard footsteps and the door opened with a creak. The man who stood behind it was taller than Gemini, but just as intimidating. He wore a black suit and white shirt, with a red tie knotted at his throat. Piercing dark eyes looked out from a thin face with a prominent sharp nose leading to a finely trimmed beard. He smelled of clove, a scent T'Challa recognized from some of the healers in Wakanda.

"You are here for Marcus," the man said.

His voice was slow and deep. It wasn't a question.

"I am," he said.

The man breathed in and seemed to grow even taller. "I am Gemini's father, and you are . . . T." He said this with curiosity, like T'Challa was some kind of strange bird or animal, a specimen for this man's collection. *How does he know who I am?*

"Yes," T'Challa said. "I am."

"Do come in, then," Mr. Jones said.

T'Challa followed Mr. Jones inside, and watched him slowly walk to the foot of the stairs. "Marcus," he called.

T'Challa took in the room around him, trying his best not to be obvious. It was like he had just stepped into a museum, but one from a place he didn't know. There were skulls of several animals that he did not recognize, African sculptures carved from wood and ivory, some with elongated necks and exaggerated features. Several clay bowls filled with flowers and red and blue powders rested on end tables. But what really took his breath away were the masks. They were everywhere—on the walls, set upon pedestals and columns, hanging from the ceiling on wires. All of them were quite strange, with leering grins and broken teeth. A standing candelabrum displayed three red candles, flickering with flame in the dim room. It smelled of dust and old books. Even though he had never been in an American home before, he knew that most probably didn't look like this.

Heavy footsteps brought him back to attention. M'Baku bounded down the stairs. Gemini wasn't with him. Mr. Jones stepped away from the stairway. M'Baku froze on the bottom step. "T.," he said. "What are you doing here?"

"I wanted to talk to you," T'Challa replied. "About . . . a class assignment."

Mr. Jones eyed them both curiously.

"C'mon," M'Baku said. "Let's go outside."

T'Challa turned to open the door—without looking at Mr. Jones—and he and M'Baku stepped outside.

Both boys began to walk—to where, T'Challa didn't know. Several moments passed in silence until he finally spoke. "What are you doing, M'Baku? Why did you join them? The Skulls, I mean. I . . . I saw the ritual."

M'Baku came to a stop. He turned to T'Challa. "You what?"

"I saw it all—the blindfolds, the skull, the oath you took. Why would you do it?"

M'Baku shook his head. "You *spied* on me?"

"I had to find out what you were doing," T'Challa confessed. "Why you've been acting so strange."

"Let me guess," M'Baku challenged him. "Your little nerd friends were with you, right?"

T'Challa swallowed back his anger.

M'Baku looked at the ground and flexed his jaw. T'Challa saw that he had on new sneakers. "Where'd you get the shoes?" he asked.

M'Baku looked up and grinned, then bounced on his toes. "Like my new kicks? Pretty dope, huh? Gemini's dad bought 'em for me. Said to consider it a favor."

"And what does he want in return?"

"Yo, Marcus!"

They both turned.

Gemini, Bicep, and a few other Skull members were headed in their direction. T'Challa recognized a new face— a girl, wearing combat boots. Her hair was drawn back in a ponytail and her face was sharp and angular, like a fox's.

"I'm out," M'Baku said, and turned to meet his friends.

"Marcus," T'Challa called.

But M'Baku didn't turn around, only headed toward Gemini with a swagger in his step.

CHAPTER TWENTY-FOUR

"So what happened?" Sheila asked the next morning. "With Marcus?"

T'Challa grimaced. "I went by to talk to him, but he didn't say much. He left when Gemini and his friends showed up. There was a girl with them this time. She had on combat boots."

Sheila's eyebrows rose. "Hmpf. Sounds like Wilhelmina Cross."

"Who's she?" T'Challa asked.

"Well, she used to be a friend of mine until we hit seventh grade. Then she started cutting classes and hanging out with people I didn't know."

"Sounds familiar," T'Challa replied.

▲ ▲ ▲

Later that day, T'Challa sat in History class, his thoughts rambling and scattered. He couldn't concentrate. He had barely slept the night before, and when he did fall asleep, he dreamed that he was walking near a deep pit bubbling with molten lava. Every time he got close to the edge his legs trembled and he wavered unsteadily, as if the pit was trying to pull him in.

The teacher was going on and on about the Battle of Gettysburg, but he might as well have been speaking gibberish. A burst of static from the PA system made T'Challa jump.

"Mr. T. Charles, please report to the principal's office. Mr. T. Charles, please proceed to the principal's office immediately."

What now? T'Challa thought.

His fellow classmates looked at him with quiet curiosity as he got up and headed for the door. T'Challa heard their hushed voices as he walked out:

What did he do?

I don't know.

His friend Marcus isn't in school.

He pushed the gossip aside and made his way to Mrs. Deacon's office.

Mr. Walker, the principal's assistant he'd met on his first day, showed him in with a tight-lipped half smile.

T'Challa took a seat and placed his hands on his knees.

Mrs. Deacon sat behind her desk and took a sip of coffee. She tapped a pencil against a sheet of paper. "Your friend Marcus hasn't been seen in school in a few days," she started. "Some of his teachers brought it to my attention. Do you have any idea where he is?"

T'Challa had no reason to lie, and he was glad of it. "I think he's staying with the Joneses," he answered.

Mrs. Deacon angled her head. "Gemini's father? Bartholomew Jones?"

Bartholomew Jones. T'Challa stored the name away for later.

"Yes," T'Challa answered. "That's all he told me."

Mrs. Deacon looked to the window for a moment. Now T'Challa had an opening, he realized. She definitely knew something about Gemini. He had to press her and find out more. "Is that weird?" he asked. "I mean—I know he should be at school. But staying with Gemini. Is that something to worry about?"

He sat back in his chair, hoping he didn't come across as too curious. The old radiator in the room clanged and then settled.

Mrs. Deacon leaned forward and rested her elbows on the wooden desk. She seemed to be struggling with something. Now was T'Challa's chance to pounce.

"Marcus is my friend," he said. "I just want to make sure he's okay."

Mrs. Deacon took another sip of coffee. She set the cup

down and looked to the window again. She turned back to him, and her face was solemn. She stood up suddenly. "If you care about your friend," she said, returning to the door, "I suggest you do everything you can to get him to come to his senses."

T'Challa was flummoxed. *Why does she sound so serious?*

"Thank you, Mrs. Deacon," he said. "I will do my best."

She didn't respond, only smiled weakly as she let T'Challa out.

She definitely knows something, T'Challa thought, as he made his way down the hallway. *She was keeping something back. What does she know about Gemini?*

T'Challa glanced at this watch. *Still fifteen minutes left in History class.*

He opened the door quietly and found students bent over their desks, scribbling furiously. There must have been a pop quiz. He closed the door behind him and took a seat. He gazed out of the window at the gray sky and the skeletons of the bare trees.

"Attention," the PA system rang out. "Attention."

Again? T'Challa thought in disbelief. *What is going on in this place?*

"Calmly proceed to the nearest side and back exits of the school in an orderly fashion. Do not use the front exit. Repeat, do not use the front exit."

The class immediately began to murmur as the announcement trailed off. Squeaking chairs and voices filled the air.

Mr. Sofio, the history teacher, stood up and raised his voice. "Class," he started, "simmer down. Quickly find your belongings and follow me. No running, please. Single file."

T'Challa joined the throng exiting the classroom. Mr. Sofio led them down through the stairwell. *What could this be about?*

T'Challa and the rest of the class took a side door exit and gathered outside near a chain-link fence. It was quiet but for the chattering of students, wondering what had interrupted another ordinary day. T'Challa stood on his toes, looking left and right.

"T.," a voice called out.

He followed the voice to Zeke, standing with Sheila a short distance away. They were probably supposed to stay with their own classes, but T'Challa slowly walked over to join them anyway. "What's happening?" he asked.

"I don't know," said Sheila.

But they soon found their answer.

Very slowly, heads started to turn. A boy T'Challa didn't know pointed toward the school entrance, which could be seen from where T'Challa stood, even though it was several hundred feet away. A quiet, almost electric buzz ran through the crowd. T'Challa squinted. Even from this distance, he could tell what it was.

There, around the double doors and on the yellowed lawn that led up to it, were at least twenty Devil's Traps, lying in wait, like some sort of bizarre omen.

CHAPTER
TWENTY-FIVE

"They wanted to make sure they weren't some kind of explosive devices or something," Sheila said. "That's what everybody's saying."

"It's the Skulls," T'Challa whispered. "Who else could it be? I mean, we saw those things at their ceremony, remember?"

There was a moment of silence.

"But what do they *do*?" Zeke demanded. "What are they used for?"

"Calling spirits," T'Challa said.

"Whose spirit?" Sheila asked.

"Those traps are around the school for a reason," T'Challa

said. "Whoever—or whatever—they're trying to summon probably has some connection to the school."

"Good point," Sheila said.

"So," T'Challa said. "What is it about this school? What could they want that's connected to South Side Middle?"

A minute or two passed while the trio sat thinking. Zeke bit his lip. Sheila squinted, like if she did it hard enough she'd get an answer.

"A teacher?" suggested Zeke.

"A student," Sheila countered, and her expression lit up. "Yeah. Maybe it's a student. Someone who went here a long time ago."

"Right," T'Challa agreed. "Someone that people back then would've looked up to. A very smart boy or girl. A leader. Gemini's obsessed with respect and proving he's important."

"We can look in old yearbooks," Sheila suggested.

"But what year?" Zeke asked. "It could be anyone, from any decade."

Silence fell again.

"Wait a minute," Zeke started, "maybe I can ask my grandmamma. She went to school here a long time ago, like way back in the 1950s. She might know something."

T'Challa slowly turned to Zeke. "Your grandmother went to school here?"

"Yeah," Zeke said.

T'Challa looked at Zeke, then to Sheila. "So where do you live, Zeke?"

Saturday morning dawned bright and warmer than usual. T'Challa felt the sun on his face, and for a moment he had a fleeting memory of Wakanda's heat and sunshine.

He found Zeke's grandmother's house easily. It was in Hyde Park, the same neighborhood where they all had pizza just a few nights before. Rows of neat houses lined the streets, each with a separate lawn and flowerbox on the porch railings, even this late in the year. He stood on the doorstep and rang the bell.

Zeke answered. "Hey, come on in, T."

T'Challa walked in and looked around. Zeke's grandmother's house was warm and inviting, certainly different from Gemini's. The whole place was bright, with a big bay window in the front room that let in generous amounts of light. Paintings hung on the walls, and vases full of flowers were placed on the dining room table. Sheila sat on the couch fiddling with her cell phone. "Hey, T.," she called, without looking up.

"Hey," he replied. "Zeke, where's your grandmother?"

Before Zeke had a chance to answer, a woman came in with a tray of cookies and other treats. She didn't look old enough to T'Challa to be a grandmother. Her hair was gray and pulled back into a bun, but her face didn't seem to have a wrinkle. *Black don't crack,* he remembered one of the kids at school saying.

"So you must be the infamous Mr. T. Charles," she said, setting down the tray. "It's nice to meet you. I'm Mrs. Dawson."

"It's nice to meet you, too," T'Challa replied.

"Ezekiel talks about you all the time," Mrs. Dawson said. "He said you're smart, and I like smart people!"

Her face lit up in a smile, and T'Challa couldn't help but do the same.

Zeke gave a sheepish grin, embarrassed.

"So," she said, and then sat down in a chair with a pattern of flowers on it. "Ezekiel said you're all working on a project about the school? Some kind of history assignment?"

"Uh, yeah," Sheila replied. "What do you remember from those days, Mrs. Dawson? When you went to school at South Side Middle?"

Mrs. Dawson leaned back in her chair. "Well, back then we didn't call it that. It was South Side Academy for Colored Children."

"Wow," said Zeke. "That's politically incorrect."

"Well," Zeke's grandmother replied, "you know things were different back then. Don't you remember my stories, baby? Colored was the *nicest* thing we were called."

T'Challa listened with a patient ear. He knew the history of black people in the United States. He still couldn't believe how they were treated during the country's founding. It was humanity at its worst, his father had told him.

"Anyway," Mrs. Dawson went on, "we had dances and socials, just like you kids today. We were all happy, even with all the trouble and strife around us."

Mrs. Dawson closed her eyes for a moment, as if remembering her childhood.

"All that changed with the fire, of course."

"Fire?" T'Challa said, leaning in.

Mrs. Dawson shook her head. "Doesn't that school tell y'all anything about its history? Somebody needs to write a book."

T'Challa nodded. Zeke reached for a cookie and stuffed it in his mouth.

"So what happened?" Sheila asked. "The fire?"

Mrs. Dawson took a sip of water and then placed the glass back on the table. "Well, they said it started in the basement. It was a tragedy. Everybody made it out alive but for one boy, poor child." She shook her head in dismay.

"Who?" Zeke asked.

"I'll never forget," Mrs. Dawson said, and then smiled sadly. "He was the prettiest boy I'd ever laid eyes on."

Zeke groaned.

"Well, he was, honey. This was before I met your grand-daddy. Everybody knew him. Everybody *respected* him."

Zeke shot T'Challa a look.

Mrs. Dawson tilted her head. "Had a curious name, that child. Vincent Dubois. Said his family was all black aristocrats." She chuckled. "Can you believe it? This boy was something else. Smart. Funny. But some girls said he was dangerous."

"Dangerous?" Sheila asked.

"Well, I never had reason to think that. He was always nice to me. Just as polite as all get-out. Used to do the strangest magic tricks."

T'Challa almost stopped breathing.

"He used to scare the little kids sometimes; used to say— and I always remembered it—'I am the Prince of Bones, and don't you forget it!'"

T'Challa's mouth went dry. He licked his lips. "Prince of Bones," he said. "Do you know what that means?"

Mrs. Dawson narrowed her eyes. "What are you children up to? I thought this was about the school."

Zeke swallowed. "It is, Grandmamma. We're just trying to find out what it was like back then."

Mrs. Dawson looked at her grandson with a skeptical eye. "Well, don't y'all go messing with stuff that's best left alone."

Now T'Challa was really curious. *Why would she say that?*

Sheila put on her best face—all bright eyes and charm. "We won't, Mrs. Dawson. So . . . about the Prince of Bones?"

Mrs. Dawson shook her head, as if growing tired of the questions. "This is the last thing I'll say about it." She took another sip of water and then set down her glass. "Well, some folks whispered that Vincent Dubois had a gang, you see. Not like today, with all the fighting and nonsense, but more like a club. A *secret* club. Called themselves the Skulls."

T'Challa's pulse raced.

Sheila dropped her phone and picked it back up. Zeke didn't say a word.

Mrs. Dawson lowered her voice, as if telling a spooky tale around a campfire. "You see, people used to say Vincent made a pact with the devil. That's why he was so pretty. Folks said he was into the dark side. Stuff that God-fearing people shouldn't be messing with. And that's why the fire took him."

There was a moment of silence.

Mrs. Dawson leaned back in her chair and blew out a breath. "Never found his body, poor child. Somebody said his burned-up bones are under the dang school."

CHAPTER
TWENTY-SIX

The bright sunlight outside did nothing to warm the trio's dark thoughts.

"The Skulls are trying to summon Vincent Dubois's spirit," T'Challa said.

"That's what they're using those Devil's Traps for," Sheila added.

"Prince of Bones," Zeke said.

The words of that night came back to T'Challa, and he said them aloud: "'I swear my life to the Skulls, in this life and the next. I swear to this oath, and may I be turned to ash if I do not abide.'"

"Well, Vincent was turned to ash, all right," Zeke said.

"That's not funny," Sheila scolded him.

"Guys," T'Challa cut in. "If Gemini and the Skulls want to summon Vincent Dubois's spirit, what will they do then? I mean, what's the purpose?"

"Maybe they think he'll give them some kind of power or something," said Zeke. "For bringing him back to the world. That's what it's like in the stories."

Sheila nodded. "I think your stories might be right for once, Zeke."

Monday came sooner than T'Challa had expected. The days were flying by, and there was still no sign of M'Baku in school.

T'Challa's watch chimed. He looked down at the device on his wrist, blinking red. His heart leapt. *It has to be Father. Who else could it be?*

He continued down the hall, but quickened his pace. He didn't want to draw attention, but he had to answer the call. Something could have happened . . . something bad.

He peeked into the open door of a classroom. Empty. He rushed inside and tapped the watch face with his index finger. A 3-D image of his father's face appeared in the air.

"Father!"

"Son," his father replied.

The king's face was worn, as if he hadn't been sleeping.

"Is everything okay?" T'Challa asked.

The Black Panther released a trembling breath. "We

were attacked two days ago. There were casualties, but we have held the invaders back. As I feared, it is Ulysses Klaw, the man of whom I spoke."

T'Challa's head spun. "Attacked? Hunter—is he . . . ?"

"Hunter is fine."

T'Challa breathed a sigh of relief. As much as Hunter plagued him, he didn't want to see him come to a bad end.

His father's face wavered in a blaze of static and then came back clear.

"T'Challa," the king said, and his voice was urgent. "You need to stay safe. You and M'Baku must remain even more on your guard now, until all of this is worked out."

T'Challa looked to the closed door and then back to the hologram. "Father," he started. "M'Baku . . . he's—"

T'Challa paused.

I can't bother him with my troubles. He's dealing with more important things.

"What?" his father asked. "What about M'Baku?"

"He's just up to his usual antics," T'Challa said suddenly. "All is well here."

The Black Panther's brow furrowed, and he gave his son an inquiring gaze. "You're the sensible one, T'Challa. Let him know what has happened. You both have to stay safe, especially now. Someone could take advantage of the turmoil here and—"

His father's voice crackled.

"Father?" T'Challa said, tapping the image. "Hello?"

The connection went dead in a blast of static.

T'Challa flopped onto his bed at the embassy. He was drained. His thoughts shifted to his father. He had to get back home.

The kingdom needed him. *When the fighting starts, I'll be here by Father's side, not running off to hide in America.*

But what could he do?

The words of the oath M'Baku took came back to him:

Darkness falls,
And He shall awaken.
Swear to Him,
And ye shall be rewarded.

Swear to whom? he wondered. *Vincent Dubois?*

T'Challa rose off the bed and walked to the safe. His father had often given him small, unexpected gifts. Perhaps there was something hidden in the box, a token of his father's affection. Now, more than ever, he needed a reminder of home.

He knelt and turned the combination, the one he came up with when he and M'Baku first arrived. He listened intently as the tumblers clicked and then released. He reached inside and took out the black box encrusted with gemstones. It opened easily on silent hinges.

The suit was on top, folded neatly. He picked it up and felt the fabric in his hands, the black material supple and soft. He set it aside and turned back to the case.

He gasped.

The bottom of the case was empty.

His heart sped up.

"No," he whispered.

He turned it upside down and shook it.

His ring was gone.

Gone.

There was only one person who could've taken it.

M'Baku.

CHAPTER
TWENTY-SEVEN

T'Challa paced back and forth in the small room. He couldn't tell Zeke or Sheila that his ring was missing. He was supposed to be an ordinary exchange student from Kenya, not a prince from Wakanda.

M'Baku wouldn't, T'Challa told himself. His friend knew the power and value of that ring. It was Vibranium, his country's most valued resource.

Why would he take it?

There was only one thing to do. He had to go to Gemini's house again.

He turned to look at his suit.

Do not wear it unless you are in an emergency.

Well, T'Challa thought, releasing a labored breath, *this is an emergency.*

T'Challa lifted the Panther suit from the velvet-lined box.

He felt the mesh of the Vibranium under his fingertips, smooth yet hard at the same time. It almost seemed like it pulsed. Like it *wanted* to be worn.

"This is the suit of the Black Panther," T'Challa whispered. "The suit of my father and his father before him."

He let the fabric fall from his hands and unfurl toward the floor.

"I have to do this," he said. "I have no choice."

He quickly changed into the suit.

His heart raced the moment his skin made contact with the Vibranium. It clung to him like an invisible glue, a bond that had its history in every Black Panther before him.

He put on his regular clothes over the suit and slipped out of the embassy, backpack in tow.

The lights, cars, and pedestrians along Michigan Avenue were a beehive of activity. People were everywhere—shuffling along in long coats, carrying shopping bags and strolling out of restaurants and stores. Street musicians sang, drummers drummed, and several people who seemed to be down on their luck asked him for money. He thought it sad that a nation as rich as America couldn't take care of their less fortunate.

He stopped for a brief moment to study a man painted

all in silver, standing on a box outside a department store. He stood motionless, with an open suitcase full of coins and bills at his feet. A shy little boy, at the urging of his mother, dropped a handful of coins into the box. The man immediately began to move like a robot, fluidly and mechanically. It was one of the strangest things T'Challa had ever seen.

He continued on his way, but this time, he did decide to take a bus. After waiting in the cold for about ten minutes, a blue-and-white city bus pulled up to the stop with a hiss. He climbed up the short steps and tapped his card against the reader. A red light flashed.

"Card's empty," the bus driver said.

T'Challa cursed himself. He looked around, embarrassed, and stuffed his hands into his pockets, but only came up with lint. People were beginning to stare. He heard a few groans from the back.

"I got ya," a voice called out.

T'Challa turned as a man got up and tapped a card against the reader.

His heart stopped.

It was the man again.

The same one he saw on that first day.

The same one he and M'Baku saw in the park.

"Thank you, sir," said T'Challa, looking at the man. He didn't know where to look—the eyepatch was distracting, and he didn't want to be rude.

"No problem," the man said, and then turned around and stepped off the bus.

T'Challa exhaled. *Who was he? He could be some sort of foreign agent working against Wakanda. But if he were an enemy, he would have tried something—a kidnapping or an assault. Maybe he's a friend of Father's. It would be just like him to have someone looking out for me in the States.*

T'Challa took a seat farther down the aisle. The man next to him had a bundle of plastic bags at his feet and seemed to be asleep, his breath coming loud and noisy. No one seemed to notice or care.

The bus came to a squeaking halt and more passengers got on. In the commotion that followed—people getting up and others getting on—T'Challa got off close to the big Greek church, still nervous and wary.

The bright lights of Michigan Avenue were replaced by streetlights and dimly lit storefronts. It was in complete contrast to the other side of the city. There were no fancy department stores or people walking out of restaurants, flipping open cell phones and hailing cabs. T'Challa thought it strange that one part of the city could be so vibrant and colorful and the other completely different. In Wakanda, everyone was treated equally and had the same opportunities, no matter who they were.

He paused.

How did he know that was true?

That was his privilege talking. He could get whatever

he wanted anytime, but it was certainly different for others. He'd seen it firsthand.

He shook his head. M'Baku was right: *You were born with a silver spoon in your mouth.*

He continued to walk, keeping his eyes peeled for any sudden movements—he didn't want to get attacked again— and ducked into a dark alley and slung off his backpack, then changed out of his street clothes. He hoisted the pack onto his shoulders.

What would happen if someone saw me in my suit?

At least it was close to the American celebration of Halloween. He could say he was in a costume.

He put on his mask and looked up. Glimpses of moonlight shone through fast-moving clouds. He slipped through the alley like a black shadow. Now he really felt powerful in the suit. The material was like a second skin. Tiny beads of light seemed to radiate from it, but they disappeared if he looked at them too long. *Perhaps it's a feature of the Vibranium.*

He spotted the griffin sculpture from a distance, even though the night was pitch-black. The streetlights were out, but he could still see clearly. *How? The suit?*

T'Challa walked around to the back of the house. It was surrounded on all sides by a chain-link fence at least six feet high. He took a deep breath, crouched low, and, in one effortless motion . . . jumped.

He landed softly, without a sound.

He couldn't believe it. He would never have been able to

do that on his own. It was definitely the suit—the Vibranium allowed him to perform a feat like this.

T'Challa looked around. A soft glow was emanating from each corner of the yard. Some sort of spotlight, he guessed.

Should I just go up and knock on the back door?

No. If M'Baku was bold enough to take his ring, he wouldn't give it back easily. T'Challa's stomach lurched. His best friend, someone he had known since childhood, had betrayed him. He still couldn't believe it.

There were no lights on inside the house. Perhaps there was no one home. He should have asked his father more about the Panther suit. He wasn't sure of all of its capabilities. He needed to be invisible. "*Stealth,*" he whispered.

T'Challa felt more than saw the suit shift to a deeper shade of black. Small wisps of light danced along the fabric and winked out. "Awesome," he whispered.

He stalked across the lawn quietly, not making a sound. He heard crickets in the grass, the sounds of insects chittering. Everything was heightened, illuminated.

A basement window looked promising. It was small but big enough for him to crawl through. T'Challa knelt. "Forgive me," he said, and kicked in the glass.

He slid through the window easily, although it was tight. Jagged pieces of glass brushed his suit, but he didn't feel the slightest tear or cut. He was reminded of the way a speckled rainbow trout slipped from his hands while he was fishing with M'Baku.

The basement was as dark as a moonless night, but T'Challa saw shapes and outlines of stairs in the near distance. He looked up. He sensed spiderwebs hanging from the wooden rafters. He walked over quietly and took one step at a time, hoping the stairs didn't creak. He was lucky. Either his weight or the suit's stealth mode prevented the old wooden stairs from making a sound.

He reached the top, took a deep breath, and pushed open the door.

He was standing in the same room as when he came to see M'Baku. It smelled of clove, old books, and dust. The masks on the wall were cast in eerie moonlight. Tall bookshelves lined the walls. He wanted, more than anything, to flip through some of the books, but he didn't have time. He had to find where M'Baku slept and search the room.

Another flight of stairs was off to the right. T'Challa moved a little more confidently. If anyone were home they would have made themselves known by now.

He paused at the top of the stairs. Several rooms ran along each wall, all with closed doors. He walked down the hallway softly, holding his breath, alert for any sudden movements. A poster on one door showed a group of boys lounging against a metal fence with crossed arms and cocky grins. "West Side Posse," T'Challa whispered, reading the large red letters. It sounded familiar. *They have hip-hop over there?* he recalled Gemini asking. *West Side Posse? Killa Krew?*

This was definitely Gemini's room.

T'Challa took a deep breath, tensed, and turned the doorknob.

Empty.

Where are Gemini and M'Baku this time of night? Probably at one of their creepy meetings, he realized.

The room was dark. He almost flipped on the light switch but thought better of it at the last second. He peered around the room: a bed, a dresser, more posters on the wall displaying musicians and sports stars, and several books on an end table. He walked over to the bedside and studied them. T'Challa was surprised to see several colorful graphic novels, the same kind of books Gemini had heckled Zeke for reading. He lifted the pile of books and set them on the bed.

An open eye stared up at him.

It was a book, the last one in the pile.

THE GRIMOIRE
OF
VINCENT DUBOIS

T'Challa's eyes widened.

He couldn't believe what he was looking at. A relic of the past, right here in Gemini's room. The cover looked to have been brown leather at one point. The edges were burned, like it had been retrieved from a fire. Some of the pages were stuck together, as if the book had been water damaged.

T'Challa carefully turned the cover. The handwriting was clear and distinct, but burned and missing in places. Bold capital letters spelled out the chapters:

THE MAN WITH NO FACE

CROW SEIZES SCORPION

THE INVISIBLE EYE

"Eye," T'Challa whispered.

He turned the page. Spots of green mold dotted the paper, but still, the slanted, neat letters could be read:

This thing called Magick is a fearsome devil, and is quick to fool those who think themselves as mighty.

The doing is in the belief, brother.

Believe, and ye shall prosper.

Your mind is the door through which all wisdom walks.

If you so believe, so do those you look upon.

Lay eyes upon your own hand, and let the words come.

Fix your eye on the one who waits.

T'Challa looked to the bottom of the page:

Carpe Noctem.

"*Carpe noctem,*" T'Challa whispered, and the Latin came to him easily: "Seize the night."

He flipped through the book. Symbols, numbers, and drawings crowded every page. *I should take it,* he considered. *Study it. No. They'd know I was here.*

T'Challa thumbed through the book again. He paused.

There, at the very back, was another page, also handwritten:

The Prince of Bones was like me. Someone destined for greatness.

We share the same beliefs.

He knew the higher mysteries, and now I will, too!

I will bring him back, and who will stop us then?

We are the Skulls!

We were right, T'Challa thought. *Right all along.* This had to be Gemini's writing. It would be just like him to add his own story to Vincent's journal, like he was preserving it for history.

T'Challa concentrated on the page again. There was more writing along the bottom:

Midnight,
Under the gibbous moon,
In the damp below,
Where the arches meet.

T'Challa cocked his head. He didn't understand it.

He set the book down, remembering why he had come here in the first place: *My ring.*

He turned away from the bedside, ready to look further.

His heart skipped.

Jangling keys.

Downstairs.

Someone had opened the door.

CHAPTER
TWENTY-EIGHT

T'Challa slid into a closet full of sneakers, gym clothes, deflated basketballs, and broken lamps. Footsteps sounded downstairs. Someone coughed. It didn't sound like a kid. It sounded like an adult.

He could hear his own breathing in the dark. He stood there, waiting for the creak of someone coming up the steps, but instead, a voice drifted up through the floorboards.

"What of the children? They have sworn to it?"

"Yes," a second man replied. "They have. Gemini did it."

T'Challa sucked in a breath. He'd recognize that deep tone anywhere. It was Gemini's father.

"Your own son?" the other voice asked in surprise.

There was a pause, and T'Challa thought he heard the sound of a cork being popped and liquid being poured into a glass. "I will not be denied," Mr. Jones said. "I have waited too long. They are expendable—mere vessels for my work."

"And the ring?"

A jolt went through T'Challa.

"Oh yes," Mr. Jones said. "The Vibranium should provide enough energy, but we shall see, won't we?"

He has my ring! T'Challa fumed, clenching his fist. *And he knows about Vibranium!*

Rage boiled in T'Challa's veins. More than anything, he wanted to rush downstairs and confront them. But he couldn't. He didn't know what he'd be facing. He had to wait.

And wait he did.

Time seemed to slow down there in the dark closet. T'Challa saw shafts of moonlight at the bottom of the door, heard the ticking of a clock and the bark of a neighbor's dog. All these sounds seemed to crystallize in his mind. It was as if he could reach out and touch them. *Feel* them. He remembered reading of how a visually impaired person's remaining senses were stronger because they had to be relied on more. That's what it felt like.

Finally, with T'Challa standing still and quiet, his breath coming slow and steady, he heard the clatter of keys through the floorboards and then footsteps. He perked up his ears. "Come," Mr. Jones's voice called. "It is time for the meeting. The Circle cannot be delayed."

T'Challa sensed the presence of someone rising from a chair. He could *feel* it, like a blood pressure cuff tightening around his arm. His father once told him that the Vibranium mesh responded to movement, alerting its wearer of possible threats.

A door opened, and then closed. The sound of footfalls echoed across the flagstones leading away from the house.

T'Challa released a long-held breath.

Whatever was happening, he had to get out.

Now.

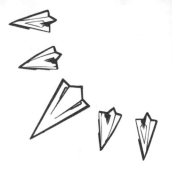

CHAPTER
TWENTY-NINE

"You broke into their house?" Sheila asked the next morning.

Red and gold leaves swirled in a circle on the football field. T'Challa shifted on the hard wooden bleachers. "I had to," he said. "Marcus . . . has something of mine."

"What is it?" Zeke asked, pushing his glasses up.

T'Challa hesitated. *I can't tell them the truth. Can I?*

But he had to tell them something. And he had to tread carefully. Mr. Jones had his ring, but he had to let Zeke and Sheila know what he'd heard without giving anything away.

"I wanted to see if I could find any clues on those Devil's Traps, but I found something else."

Sheila and Zeke leaned in.

"A grimoire," T'Challa said, "an old journal belonging to Vincent Dubois. It was waterlogged and burned. There were spells in it, and one of them was for something called the Invisible Eye, but it was written in a very old-fashioned kind of way, and I couldn't make anything of it. It was all about believing in what you were doing."

He swallowed.

"But Gemini wrote in it, too. He said that he and Vincent were the same—that they were both destined for greatness. He said that he was going to bring Vincent back, and learn the higher mysteries."

"We were right," Sheila whispered.

There was a moment of silence.

"There was a strange phrase he'd written in the very back," T'Challa continued, "but I couldn't make any sense of it. 'Midnight, under the gibbous moon, in the damp below, where the arches meet.'"

"What the heck does that mean?" Zeke asked.

"I don't know," T'Challa replied.

Sheila silently mouthed the words, considering.

T'Challa looked out toward the woods beyond the football field. Gray clouds rolled in the distance. *You can trust them*, a voice in his head urged him. *You're all working together. You've got enough secrets.* "There's more," he said.

Sheila raised her eyebrows. She turned to Zeke and then back to T'Challa.

T'Challa swallowed again. "I heard Mr. Jones talking to

another man. They said something about getting children to swear on something. Gemini supposedly did it."

"Like the ritual!" Zeke exclaimed. "He made those kids swear on that book!"

"'Darkness falls,'" Sheila whispered, her voice almost trembling. "'And He shall awaken.'"

"'Swear to Him,'" T'Challa added, "'and ye shall be rewarded.'" He paused and looked at both of them. "Mr. Jones is doing something really evil. Something deadly. Whatever Gemini and the Skulls have planned is nothing compared to this. He said something about a circle, and that the children were expendable, and that he would not be denied."

Silence fell again, but for the raucous chatter of crows in the trees.

"That means Mr. Jones is going to do something to *them*," Zeke said.

T'Challa nodded. "You're right, Zeke. We have to help them before it's too late."

Sheila crossed her arms. "I'm not helping Gemini Jones. No way."

Zeke remained quiet—unsure of what to say, it seemed to T'Challa. "We probably *have* to help them," he finally said. "Even if we don't want to."

Sheila remained adamant. "Zeke, remember that time Gemini and his friends got that new boy lost in the woods? And when they tried to stuff your head down the—"

"I know. I know," Zeke interrupted. "Don't remind me. They're definitely not nice. But who knows what Mr. Jones is up to? It could be serious, and if something bad really *does* happen, how could we live with ourselves?"

"We have to at least *talk* to Gemini," T'Challa suggested. Sheila scowled.

"When?" Zeke asked. "How?"

T'Challa sat for a moment, thinking. He bit his lip. "I don't know," he finally said, "but whatever we do, we have to do it soon. Mr. Jones could strike at any time."

A shadow passed over Sheila's face.

"What?" T'Challa asked. "What is it?"

"Gibbous," Sheila said, as if she were in a trance. "I remember now. It's when the moon's nearly full, but doesn't cast a lot of light."

"And when is that?" Zeke asked.

Sheila swallowed. "In two days."

CHAPTER THIRTY

T'Challa knew what he had to do, but he wasn't looking forward to it. "Here goes," he said, and walked toward Gemini's table. "Just let me do the talking."

Sheila and Zeke looked at each other skeptically. "Yes, sir," Sheila said.

T'Challa was surprised to find the Skulls in the cafeteria. It seemed that they had their own schedule when it came to attending school. M'Baku was there, along with the usual crew, but this time, Wilhelmina Cross sat with them. "Look who it is," she said, as T'Challa approached the table. "And you brought the nerds with you."

The Skulls looked up and considered T'Challa and his friends. Zeke and Sheila remained quiet, but both wore scowls.

"I've heard about you," Wilhelmina said. "Marcus said you spied on us. In the woods."

The night of the strange ritual flashed through T'Challa's mind.

"Better be careful," Wilhelmina said with a sneer. "You never know what you're gonna see."

"Maybe a ghost," Deshawn said.

"Boo!" Bicep crowed.

The Skulls all laughed, except for Gemini, who only rapped his knuckles on the table.

T'Challa looked at M'Baku. *He stole my ring. I can't believe it. My best friend.*

"I need to tell you something," T'Challa said quickly.

Every set of eyes at the table fell on him.

"And what would that be?" Gemini finally said. "You're sorry for poking your nose in other people's business?"

"I know what I did," T'Challa said. "The . . . the spying, and I'm sorry."

"Sorry didn't do it," Gemini said. "You did."

"You have to listen to me," T'Challa persisted. "Something bad is going to happen. And soon. You have to be careful. I think your father's planning something."

Gemini burst up from his chair.

"*What?* What'd you say, Africa? What do *you* know about my pop?"

T'Challa stepped back. "I just know. When I came to see . . . Marcus the other day, I had a feeling. You have to be careful. Something bad is coming."

"Yeah," Wilhemina said. "Something bad *is* comin' if you don't get to steppin'."

There was nervous laughter from Deshawn and Bicep. M'Baku was expressionless. T'Challa didn't know if it was guilt or fear.

Gemini stood just a few inches from T'Challa's face. "You know something, T. Charles? I'm about tired of your mess."

And then he swung.

T'Challa ducked and sprang back up, then pushed hard with both hands against Gemini's chest.

Gemini fell back into the table, sending trays and glasses crashing.

Heads began to turn. *Fight! Fight! Fight!* rang throughout the cafeteria as a hundred or more students rushed to the commotion. Cell phones came out of pockets.

"Stop!" Zeke and Sheila shouted at the same time.

Gemini picked himself up and charged at T'Challa again. T'Challa knew he could take him. Gemini had no grace or skill, just brute strength.

He stepped aside as Gemini flung out his right leg,

trying to kick, but instead, the leader of the Skulls went down in a heap, slipping in a puddle of spilled milk. A few students in the crowd began to laugh.

Gemini bolted up and charged again. T'Challa stepped aside, but tripped, and his legs went out from under him. Wilhemina Cross smiled and drew her leg back under the table.

Gemini used T'Challa's moment of distraction to lunge. He dove on top of him, pinning the young prince to the ground. Gemini brought a fist down on T'Challa's nose. T'Challa was stunned. It felt like a thousand tiny needles had pierced him.

T'Challa saw a glimpse of M'Baku there in the crowd, stone-faced. He thought of calling out for help, but his friend was truly lost to him now.

T'Challa pushed up on his elbows with all his strength and hurled Gemini off.

Tweet!!!!!

The throng parted as Mr. Blevins pushed through the crowd, whistle dangling from his mouth. "Break it up!" he shouted. *Tweet!!!!!* "Break it up *now*!"

Gemini rose to his feet. "Keep my pop's name out of your mouth!" he shouted.

T'Challa got up. The back of his pants were wet from rolling around in spilled milk. Everyone was staring at him.

"Alright," Mr. Blevins said. "Everybody settle down." He turned to T'Challa and Gemini. A vein throbbed on his forehead. "I don't even wanna know what it was about, so spare me the excuses. If it happens again, you're both running twenty laps around the school. Got it?"

T'Challa nodded.

"I hear you," Gemini said, breathing hard.

"Beat it," Mr. Blevins said. "Both of you knuckleheads."

T'Challa turned to leave, but not before M'Baku shot him a glance.

T'Challa saw nothing behind his eyes, just a blank stare, like he was wearing a mask and the real M'Baku was missing.

Could that be? T'Challa wondered again. *Is Gemini behind this? Did he put a spell on him?*

"You okay, T'Challa?"

T'Challa jumped. He looked at Zeke. "What did you call me?"

Zeke cocked his head, curious. Sheila's forehead wrinkled.

"I called you T.," Zeke said slowly. "What did you think I said?"

T'Challa squinted, still breathing hard from exertion. He could have sworn that Zeke called him by his true name. *Do they know somehow?*

He was tired. That was it. He needed a break. "Nothing," he said. "Just hearing things, I guess."

Zeke turned and cast a questioning glance at Sheila.

CHAPTER
THIRTY-ONE

T'Challa got up to answer the door. His nose was still stinging.

Clarence the concierge cocked his head and leaned in. "Ouch," he said. "I bet that smarts."

"I'll be okay," T'Challa said.

Clarence handed T'Challa the ice pack he had called for. T'Challa pressed it up to his nose. Clarence came half-way into the room and peered around. "What happened to your friend?" he asked. "The higher-ups here at the embassy didn't give us your names, but we were told you were very important guests."

T'Challa hesitated. *Is he fishing for information, or just being a little nosy?*

"Anyway," Clarence continued. "I haven't seen the two of you together in a while, and I was wondering."

T'Challa flopped down in a chair. "He has some issues he's working out."

"Oh," Clarence said. "Anything I can do to help?"

"I don't think so," T'Challa answered.

"Do let me know if that changes," Clarence said.

"I will," said T'Challa.

Clarence took one last look around. "Well," he said, straightening his suit jacket. "I should be getting back downstairs, then."

"Thank you," T'Challa said. "For the ice pack."

"Not a problem," Clarence answered. "And, by the way, I know a good gym, if you ever want to learn some boxing moves."

T'Challa grimaced as Clarence left the room.

He laid his head back and closed his eyes. His nose still hurt, and the ice pack just made it a *cold* hurt. Gemini was a stubborn fool. T'Challa had tried to warn him, and he hadn't listened.

What of the children? They have sworn to it?

Midnight, under the gibbous moon, in the damp below, where the arches meet.

The Vibranium should provide enough energy, but we shall see, won't we?

What did Bartholomew Jones want with Vibranium?

T'Challa opened his eyes. He was exhausted, and he felt it in every muscle. He let out a long, winded breath. He needed to rest, just for a minute, and then get back to figuring out the mysterious clues of Mr. Jones.

RIN-N-N-G-G-G-G!

T'Challa jumped.

It was the phone.

He caught his breath. He'd never even heard it ring before. *It could be Father, but he wouldn't call on a regular old phone. Then again, it could be the strange man from the bus. Maybe I was followed again!*

Another ring shattered T'Challa's thoughts, sending his heart racing. He picked up the receiver. "Hello?"

"Yes, this is Clarence again, at the front desk. I'm sorry to disturb you. It seems you have . . . *guests.*" There was a pause and muffled voices. "Zeke and . . . Sheila? They're looking for a Mr. T. Charles."

T'Challa pulled the phone away from his ear and pressed it to his chest. *How?* he wondered. How was this possible? He raised the phone back to his ear.

"There's no other guest in the embassy by that name," Clarence continued, "but their description sounds like you."

Thousands of tiny pinpricks raced up the back of T'Challa's neck.

"*Hello?*" he heard faintly over the speaker.

T'Challa silently counted to five. He raised the phone back to his ear. "Let them up," he said.

A minute later, Zeke and Sheila were standing in T'Challa's room.

"How did you find me?" T'Challa asked.

"This is an embassy," Zeke said, taking in the room. "Why in the world would you be staying at an embassy?"

"Well," Sheila said. "He *is* from Africa." She shot a look at T'Challa. "At least that's what he says."

"Guys," T'Challa said, and loudly swallowed. His palms were sweating. "How. Did. You. Find. Me?"

Sheila and Zeke looked at each other. "We followed you," Zeke said. "I knew there was something strange going on. I couldn't figure out why the first time I met you, you caught the 134, instead of taking the 76 down Michigan Avenue."

So much for being secretive, T'Challa scolded himself.

"Plus," Sheila said, "Zeke and I caught the bus behind you from school. We followed you back here."

"*And,*" Zeke went on, "I've counted the amount of times you've dodged the question about where you live. You said you had an uncle on Michigan Avenue. So why didn't Marcus stay with *you?* Why would he be staying with a host family? And that watch of yours—"

"Enough," T'Challa said wearily. He sat on the bed and put his head in his hands. "*Enough.*"

He knew this moment was coming. He just didn't know it would be now. "No more lies," he whispered aloud.

Zeke glanced at Sheila.

T'Challa raised his head and looked at both of them. Zeke and Sheila had proved themselves as friends. *I can trust them. I have to.*

He rose off the bed. He couldn't believe what he was about to do. But he was doing it. He had to make his own decisions. "What I'm going to show you, you're not going to believe," he said.

"Try us," Zeke countered.

"Here goes," T'Challa whispered.

T'Challa walked to the safe, knelt down, and turned the combination: 2, 1, 19, 20: BAST—the name of the Panther God and his cat back home. No wonder M'Baku guessed it. He knew how much he loved that cat. *How could I have been so thoughtless?*

"What do you have in there?" Sheila ventured, voice wavering. "Please don't tell me you have a gun."

"Of course he doesn't have a gun," said Zeke. And then: "Do you have a gun?"

"No," T'Challa said, and then stood up. "But I have this."

He turned around. The mask covered his eyes.

"Uh, you're a cat burglar?" Zeke joked.

"No," he said. "I'm the son of the Black Panther. My name is T'Challa."

CHAPTER
THIRTY-TWO

"I can't believe it," Zeke said, pacing back and forth in the small embassy room. "I can't *freaking* believe it!"

"I knew there was something different about you," Sheila added, shaking her head. "I just knew it."

Zeke stopped his pacing and rounded on her. "Then why didn't you ever say anything?"

"I'm not saying I knew *who* he was, just that he was different."

"Who else knows?" Zeke asked, turning back to T'Challa.

"Just you two. And M'Baku, of course."

"So that's his name," Sheila whispered.

"You're from . . . Wakanda," Zeke said, still amazed.

"It's real. I can't believe I'm standing here talking to the Black Panther."

"I'm not the Black Panther *yet*," T'Challa said. "That's my father. A lot has to happen before that day comes."

Father.

T'Challa had broken his command to stay hidden. The kingdom was under attack, and here he was, far from home, revealing his identity.

"Wait a minute," Zeke said. "You're a prince. *A prince!* Shouldn't we kneel or something? Like, kiss your hand or whatnot?"

Sheila laughed. "Uh . . . *not.*"

"I don't think that's necessary," T'Challa assured him. "But you have to keep this a secret. If my father ever found out that I revealed myself, well, I don't know what would happen."

Zeke stared hard at T'Challa.

"What?" T'Challa asked. "What now?"

"You have a suit, right? Like a real Super Hero?"

Sheila waggled her eyebrows. "C'mon then. Let's see it."

T'Challa sighed. *No need to hide now.* He walked back to the safe and withdrew his suit from the box. He handed it to Zeke, who took it into his hands carefully, the same way T'Challa had when his father had given it to him. He felt another pang of guilt—a sharp jolt to the stomach.

Zeke's eyes almost popped out of his head as he felt the

fabric. "This is Wakandan tech," he said, as if in a daze. "Like your watch, right?"

"Right," T'Challa answered guiltily.

"What watch?" Sheila asked.

T'Challa grimaced. He just knew his little display with the watch was going to come back and haunt him. Didn't matter now, though. They knew everything anyway.

He thrust out his arm. Zeke and Sheila leaned in. "What's it do?" Sheila asked.

T'Challa tapped the screen. "Lots of things."

A pulsating red light began to glow within the opaque, black surface. After a moment, tiny particles, like dust caught in a sunbeam, rose from T'Challa's wrist and took on a three-dimensional shape. It was a cube, which rose in the air and rotated on one corner. Zeke and Sheila looked on, mouths agape.

At least I don't have to lie anymore, T'Challa thought, his guilt tinged with relief. "Guys," he said, swiping his hand through the projection, which then disappeared. Zeke's and Sheila's eyes widened even more. "Now that we're all here, we've got to figure out what to do."

"Right," Sheila agreed.

"We know Mr. Jones is planning something," T'Challa said, "but what?"

"'Midnight,'" Zeke recited, "'under the gibbous moon, in the damp below, where the arches meet.'"

T'Challa tapped a bead on his Kiyomo Bracelet. A tablet-size screen appeared in the air in front of him. He waved his hand over it and watched it float to the wall above the TV. Then it expanded.

"What the—?" Zeke said.

"And I thought the watch was cool," Sheila said under her breath.

"This is a Kiyomo Bracelet," T'Challa said, holding up his wrist. He had to admit, it did feel good to show off. Just a little. "It's different from the watch, and more of an everyday accessory."

"I thought it was just a fashion statement," Sheila said.

"Every Wakandan has one," T'Challa said. "They're used for all kinds of things." He grinned. "Like deep searches."

He walked toward the projection and tapped the screen.

"What is your query?" a pleasant female voice inquired.

"Bartholomew Jones," he said. "All data."

Instead of a page of text showing search results, a black circle appeared on the screen. The bottom edge of the circle began to glow red.

"What's it doing?" Sheila asked, leaning into the screen.

"It's searching world servers for anything to do with Bartholomew Jones," T'Challa replied.

"That's not Google," Sheila said.

"Far from it," T'Challa answered.

The automated voice spoke again:

"Result: Bartholomew Jones. Born 1975, Chicago. Antiques collector and former ancient-religions scholar. Frequent visitor to the continent. Holds several passports for African countries."

"So he was in Africa," T'Challa said. "Interesting."

"But what was he doing there?" Zeke asked.

"I don't know yet," T'Challa replied.

"That language I translated was Old Nubian," Sheila said. "Maybe ask where it's spoken?"

T'Challa didn't answer but nodded at Sheila. "New search," he said, now walking about the room. "Languages. Old Nubian. Places spoken."

The circle went back to black and began to pulse red. Zeke pushed up his glasses, not taking his eyes from the technological marvel in front of him.

"Old Nubian. Archaic, defunct language. No known first-language users in the world."

"Hmpf," muttered Sheila. She drummed her fingers on her knee. "You said some of the Old Nubian words sounded familiar. Remember? They must've been root words that worked their way into other African languages."

T'Challa kept nodding, as if listening and thinking at the same time. "New search," he announced. "Bartholomew

Jones . . . *Vibranium*." He turned to look at Zeke and Sheila. "Search Wakandan servers only."

Zeke's mouth formed an O at the mention of T'Challa's home country.

"Can *anyone* search Wakanda data?" Zeke asked.

"That would be difficult," T'Challa said. "This technology was invented there and responds only to biometrics. That's why I touched the screen before searching."

"Uh, okay," Zeke said.

They all waited while the screen ran through results. T'Challa tensed.

The screen displayed an image of the Wakandan flag marked with a stamp:

CLASSIFIED: ACCESS CODE REQUIRED

There was a moment of silence.

"Classified," T'Challa murmured, and then stared at Zeke and Sheila. "What does Gemini's dad have to do with Wakanda?"

CHAPTER
THIRTY-THREE

Sheila stood up. "Is there any way to break into that file? Like, a secret password or something?"

T'Challa grimaced. *This is Wakandan national security. I can't just break into it.*

Or can I?

It was important. He could tell his father—tell him what was really happening—but . . .

The King of Wakanda had enough worries at the moment.

I have to do this on my own. I can't run to Father with every problem. I have to lead someday.

"I'm not sure," he finally answered.

Zeke's eyes were permanently wide. He looked at Sheila, and then T'Challa, as if he had just come to a sudden revelation. "This is like, a secret mission. I'm in an embassy, talking about breaking into a top secret file with the Black Panther. Like in a graphic novel."

Sheila smiled and shook her head.

"Zeke," T'Challa said wearily. "I'm not the Black Panther, remember? That's my father, the King of Wakanda."

"But still," Zeke said. "You *will* be the Black Panther someday."

It dawned on T'Challa once again that what he was doing could put his claim to the throne in jeopardy. He sat down on the edge of the bed.

In the end, it didn't matter. He was in too far now. He swallowed. "Do you guys have any place to be? Say, for the next few hours?"

"No," Zeke and Sheila said at the same time.

"Good," T'Challa said. "I think we're going to have a long night." He picked up the phone to dial room service. "Who likes pizza?"

Over the next several hours, amid pizza boxes, bottles of soda, and chocolate bars, the trio brainstormed on how to break the code.

"Passwords?" Sheila ventured.

"No," T'Challa said. "That's too simple. All the files have encryption keys. There's no way to configure them."

"Well, did you try a brute-force attack?"

T'Challa swallowed. "A what?"

"It's a way of using another computer to get at encrypted files. There's an app for it."

"I never knew you knew so much computer stuff," Zeke said.

"That's because your head's always buried in a book," Sheila replied. "Not that that's a bad thing," she added with a half smile. She took out her tablet and quickly typed in some numbers and letters in the search bar. "Got it," she said.

"Got what?" asked T'Challa.

"The program that will help me decrypt the file."

T'Challa smiled. "Well, go for it," he said.

Sheila typed and murmured to herself, took long gulps of soda, and shook her head back and forth several times as she worked. Every now and then she'd set the tablet down and scribble something on a piece of paper.

T'Challa's thoughts drifted. Not only had he revealed his true identity, he was now in the midst of what could be called treason. *Treason*. He took a deep breath.

Sheila kept working while Zeke peppered T'Challa with questions:

"Where does Vibranium come from?"

"Exactly where in Africa *is* Wakanda, anyway?"

"Can you fly?"

T'Challa trod carefully. He didn't want to give away

more than he needed to, but Sheila unknowingly came to his rescue before he had a chance.

"Got it," she announced.

T'Challa rose from his seat.

"Bring up the search page again," Sheila ordered him.

T'Challa tapped his Kiyomo Bracelet and the screen appeared. The classified file hung in the air—taunting them, he thought.

"Okay," Sheila said, "type this string of numbers into the search bar."

T'Challa typed in what seemed like random zeroes and ones for what felt like minutes. "Are you sure this is right?" he asked during a pause, when Sheila reached for a drink of water.

"I hope so," she said. "It's binary code, and should unlock the sequence."

T'Challa typed in more zeroes and ones. Zeke bit his fingernails and watched.

"Last one," Sheila said. "Zero, one, one, zero, one."

T'Challa stopped his typing.

Everyone took a deep breath.

"Enter," Sheila said.

T'Challa's finger hovered over the screen. His heart sped up. "Here goes," he said.

He pressed ENTER.

For a moment, nothing happened. They all waited, holding their breath.

But then . . .

The Wakandan flag faded and was replaced by a picture of a man and lots of text.

T'Challa knew the face.

It was Bartholomew Jones.

"Yes!" Zeke shouted.

Sheila blew out a long and deserved breath.

T'Challa looked more closely at the screen. Under the head shot of Bartholomew Jones was a report on his activities:

Bartholomew Jones
D.O.B.: 3/10/1975
Nationality: American
First visit to Wakanda: 2000
Reason for visit: Scientific inquiry into Vibranium

T'Challa paused. "So he was looking for Vibranium." He continued to read down the page:

Colluded with fringe Wakandans called the Circle of Nine.

"Circle of Nine?" T'Challa said.

"What is it?" asked Zeke.

"Who are they?" Sheila added.

T'Challa focused on the screen in front of him.

Circle of Nine: Banned group of Wakandan mystics and fringe scientists / Some known as former PHOTON employees / Wanted Vibranium for research into dimensional portals, but request was denied.

"Oh my God," Sheila said.

"Portals?" Zeke questioned.

"What's PHOTON?" T'Challa asked.

"It's a scientific research center in Europe," Sheila said. "They invented something called the Mass Photon Accelerator."

T'Challa and Zeke gave her blank stares.

"What does it do?" T'Challa asked.

"It helps them run experiments to look for something they call the God Particle—trying to find out how life in the universe began."

"That sounds pretty cool," Zeke said.

"Well," Sheila continued, "some people say they're messing with stuff they shouldn't be—trying to split atoms and other things. They say it could lead to another Big Bang."

"Uh, guys," T'Challa said, turning away from the screen, "remember when I said Mr. Jones said something about a circle? It must have been this. The Circle of Nine. They wanted Vibranium."

My ring. I never told them.

"There's something else," he said.

Zeke's eyebrows rose.

"That night I broke into Gemini's house, I was looking for something."

"You were looking for Marcus," Sheila said. "I mean M'Baku. You said he had something of yours."

"Yes. That's right. But there's more to it. I think he stole a ring of mine. A *Vibranium* ring, and now Mr. Jones has it. I overheard him when I was in the closet. He said, 'The Vibranium should provide enough energy, but we shall see.'"

"You have a Vibranium ring?" Zeke asked.

"Yes," T'Challa replied. "My father gave it to me. In the wrong hands, that Vibranium could be dangerous."

Silence hung thick in the room.

"We have to get it back," Zeke said.

"I know," T'Challa said. "And we will."

CHAPTER
THIRTY-FOUR

T'Challa woke to empty pizza boxes, half-full soda bottles, and the smell of garlic and cheese. "Ugh," he moaned.

And then it hit him:

Midnight. Under the gibbous moon, in the damp below, where the arches meet.

He buried his face in the pillow.

What of the children? They have sworn to it?

Cold gray light from outside spread into the room. It seemed to creep into T'Challa's bones and mind. *I told them,* he thought. *I told Zeke and Sheila who I am.*

I hope I did the right thing.

T'Challa turned away from his locker. A boy passed by dressed as a medieval knight, carrying a sword made of foil. "What the . . . ?" T'Challa whispered under his breath.

The knight was followed by a girl in an astronaut costume, complete with a giant see-through helmet. Next came witches and warlocks, cavemen and cowboys, and what could only have been characters from books and movies that T'Challa had never seen. They ranged from the gruesome to the downright ridiculous.

Halloween, he suddenly remembered.

"Hey."

T'Challa spun in the opposite direction. A small figure in a black cape and red pants stood in front of him. A domino mask ringed his eyes. "Zeke?" T'Challa ventured.

"I'm not Zeke," the figure said. "I'm the Black Panther's sidekick. Red Lightning!"

"Shh!" T'Challa hissed, looking around warily.

Zeke was joined by Sheila, who looked Zeke up and down. "*Really?*" she said.

"And who are *you* supposed to be?" Zeke asked her.

"Just a girl," Sheila said, leaning against a locker and examining her fingernails. "Expert in STEM, computer hacker, and all-around bad girl."

Even Zeke smiled at that.

Sheila gave a sly smile. "Hey," she said. "I've got intel."

They ducked into an empty classroom, and Sheila placed

her silver briefcase on a table. She clicked the hinges open and drew out a stack of papers. "I was thinking," she started, "after Zeke and I left the embassy. Zeke's grandmother said there was a fire in the basement of the school, right?"

"Right," T'Challa replied.

"Well, if that's where Vincent Dubois died, it makes sense that it might be where the Skulls are going to do the summoning."

"Good thinking," T'Challa said. "Gemini said he would bring Vincent back. And where he died is probably the place to do it."

T'Challa paused. He couldn't believe that he was seriously talking about dead spirits and summonings.

"But we're trying to stop *Mr. Jones* at this point," Zeke said. "Not Gemini. He's the Big Bad, right?"

"Right," Sheila countered, and then waited, it seemed to T'Challa, for someone to figure out what she was thinking.

"Ah," said T'Challa. "I see. Mr. Jones will be wherever the Skulls are. That's how he's going to . . . do whatever he has planned."

"Exactly," said Sheila. She rooted and shuffled through more papers.

T'Challa glanced at the clock above the desk. They had about ten minutes before their next classes started.

"I pulled the school blueprints off the internet when I got home," Sheila said. "Here." She smoothed out a sheet of paper and pointed to a spot. "This is an entrance to the basement. It's where the custodians keep all the lawn mowers and stuff. If we can get in through there, we can take the stairs right down to the basement." She pointed to another spot on the plan. "Right *here*." T'Challa noticed her fingernails were painted blue with little white stars.

He angled his head and looked at the spot. "You think this could be the place? In the damp below, where the arches meet?"

"Maybe," Sheila replied.

"That door would be locked after school hours," T'Challa said. "You're not saying we'd have to—"

"Break in?" Zeke suggested. He leaned back. "Well, we're students here, so technically, we wouldn't *really* be breaking in, right?"

T'Challa hesitated. "We could hide and wait till school is over, then go from there."

Sheila slowly shook her head. "I'm not going to hide in a closet for hours until all the teachers leave. How would we know when the coast was clear?"

Zeke looked at Sheila and nodded. "What she said."

She did have a point, T'Challa realized. "Okay," he said. "We'll just meet there and get in somehow."

"How?" Zeke asked.

T'Challa smiled. "I'll find a way."

The rest of the day, T'Challa was on edge. Whenever he saw Zeke or Sheila it seemed like they were looking at him in a whole new light. He wasn't T. Charles anymore. He was T'Challa of Wakanda to them.

T'Challa watched the clock move slowly during each class. Tonight was the night—the night of the gibbous moon. What did Bartholomew Jones have planned?

The alarm bell blared loud and sudden, startling T'Challa from his thoughts. He gathered his books from his French class and headed out into the hallway. His phone chimed. He looked down at his wrist and rushed outside. It had to be his father calling, or—it suddenly occurred to him—someone calling with *news* of his father. He just hoped it wasn't bad.

He pushed past crowds of kids milling in the hall and headed for the exit. As much as he wanted to answer at that very moment, he had to get a safe distance away before using tech that could cause attention.

He pushed the heavy door open and jogged over to the football field. A flock of birds leapt up and flew away at his approach. As he reached the chain-link fence, he tapped his finger to the screen and turned his back to the school. If anyone was watching, it would look like he was leaning against the fence, staring into the woods.

A hologram of his father's face appeared. T'Challa closed his eyes for a brief moment, relieved. "Father," he said. "Are you okay? What is happening in Wakanda?"

"We have driven the invaders back," his father replied.

"For now. They breached the Vibranium Mound, but our forces held them at bay."

"Good," T'Challa said, proud of his father. "I knew we would win."

"It is only the first strike in a battle, my son," the Black Panther said. "I fear there will be many more attempts. We captured Ulysses Klaw but he escaped. He seems very determined to use Vibranium to build some sort of sonic weapon."

A blur of static flashed across the screen and quickly faded. "T'Challa," his father said. "How is M'Baku?"

T'Challa stiffened. *I can't tell him anything. This is my mission. I have to do it on my own.* "He's . . . better. We're both doing fine, Father."

The Black Panther's face grew skeptical. "Be careful, T'Challa. Do not reveal your identity. There could still be danger abroad. Do you understand?"

"Yes," T'Challa said, and almost visibly winced.

A moment of silence passed between them. T'Challa looked around. The wind was rising, stirring leaves around his feet.

He did understand, but he had already broken his promise.

CHAPTER THIRTY-FIVE

T'Challa stood in front of the mirror, the Panther suit in his hands. Once again, he felt as if the suit *wanted* to be worn. His fingers tingled as he touched the fabric. His heartbeat sped up, and his chest rose and fell with each breath he took.

He slipped into the suit.

He felt powerful. Royal. He turned to and fro in front of the mirror. He felt as if he were playacting. But he wasn't. This was *real*.

"I'm not the Black Panther yet," he said, looking at his face in the mirror, "but I promise I won't let Wakanda down."

He walked out of the bathroom, and into the embassy bedroom.

"Wow," Zeke said. "You look like . . . a Super Hero."

"Well, he is," Sheila said, smiling. She rooted around in her silver briefcase and then shut the hinges with a resounding click. Zeke stood in front of the mirror, posing in his Red Lightning outfit. Sheila looked at him and shook her head, but behind her eyes a smile took shape.

"Tell me about Vibranium," Sheila asked.

"It crashed as a meteor in Wakanda long ago," T'Challa started. "It's the rarest metal on earth, and it absorbs energy but can also release it."

"Interesting," Sheila said. "So if it stores energy, it can be used as a weapon, right?"

T'Challa paused. *A weapon?* "I think so," he said, not saying anything about the news his father had told him earlier—that Ulysses Klaw had plans for some kind of sonic weapon. "In Wakanda, it's closely guarded at all times from smugglers and thieves."

Sheila nodded. "What's it like?" she asked. "Your . . . homeland?"

T'Challa released a sigh. "It's beautiful. The forests are green and lush, the lakes and rivers crystal clear. Even the air itself is special."

He felt a pang in his stomach just thinking of home. He was worried about his father and friends. But his father said that the battle was at a pause. *Please keep them all safe,* he prayed. *Even . . . Hunter.*

Sheila seemed to pick up on T'Challa's worries. "We'll get it back," she said. "Your ring."

T'Challa nodded. "It's M'Baku I'm most worried about."

What he said was true. Although his father would be deeply upset if there was a piece of Vibranium out in the larger world, a friend and citizen of Wakanda was irreplaceable.

He had to succeed. And then get back home. If Wakanda was still under threat of war, he had to be there with his father.

T'Challa put his street clothes back on over his suit, which was so light and thin it felt like he wasn't wearing it.

Sheila turned to Zeke. "You're really going to wear that?"

"Uh, *yeah*," Zeke said with an edge. "It's like cosplay, but for real."

"What's cosplay?" T'Challa asked, stuffing his mask in his backpack and then hoisting it onto his shoulders.

"More like nerdplay," Sheila teased.

"I'll tell you later," Zeke said. "When we're . . . done with all this." He gulped, and for the first time, T'Challa saw doubt flash across his face.

"You don't have to do this," T'Challa said gently. "M'Baku is my friend. I can't just stand by and let it happen—whatever *it* is. Not to him or to anyone else. But I understand if you don't want to go any further."

"*What?*" Sheila said. "I'm doing this because you're *my*

friend. And that's what friends do, right, T'Challa? Help one another."

T'Challa paused. It was the first time either of them had used his real name. "Yeah," Zeke chimed in. "One for all, and all for one, and all that."

T'Challa smiled. That's what he and M'Baku used to say to each other. However this all ended, he thought, he had definitely made good friends here in America. He looked at both of them and released a breath. "Ready?"

Outside, Michigan Avenue was bustling, but with a cold wind that whipped between the skyscrapers. Every now and then a group of costumed partygoers strolled by, completely oblivious to the cold, it seemed to T'Challa.

The bus ride to South Side Middle School was uneventful, except for a few teenagers dressed in costumes, who laughed uncontrollably for some reason T'Challa couldn't explain.

The trio walked through the empty parking lot. It felt strange to T'Challa to be at the school this late. A few solitary cars sat in the parking lot like sleeping beasts.

Sheila led them to the corner of the school that she had indicated on the blueprint. A few narrow white steps led down to a door. T'Challa couldn't believe that he was really going to break in.

Zeke reached out for the door handle and groaned.

"What?" Sheila questioned, stepping forward to look for herself.

"Great," Zeke said in frustration. "It needs a key card."

"Actually," T'Challa said, "that's better."

He rolled up his sleeve.

"How's your super–Google watch going to unlock a door?" Sheila asked.

"Like this," T'Challa said, and then typed a sequence of numbers into the watch face. "I need a piece of paper."

Zeke took off his pack and ripped a piece of paper from his notebook.

"Tear off a small piece," T'Challa told him.

Zeke followed T'Challa's request silently, and handed it back.

T'Challa took it and folded it in half, then slid it through the magnetic strip of the security lock several times.

"What in the world?" Zeke questioned.

T'Challa took the paper and then laid it on the watch face. "Unmask," he said.

Zeke and Sheila watched in fascination as a blinking red light glowed beneath the paper. "C'mon," T'Challa whispered in anticipation. The light changed from red to green, followed by a chime.

"Yes!" T'Challa whispered.

He lifted the paper from the watch face and slid it back through the strip on the security lock.

Click.

A red dot blinked on the black box.

"We're in," he said.

Zeke's mouth hung open. "Uh, do you think I can get one of those watches?"

"I doubt it," T'Challa said, and pushed open the door.

The walls that led down to the basement of the school were covered in a mosaic of black and white tiles. Hissing steam and the sound of clanking pipes filled the air. Beads of water clung to the tiles.

T'Challa placed his foot on the bottom step. Ahead of him was nothing but darkness. "Wait a minute," he said, and his voice carried in the dark. He slung off his backpack and then slipped out of his street clothes, revealing his suit—the suit of the Black Panther. He stuffed his clothes in his backpack. The Vibranium mesh in the suit winked in the darkness, like stars.

"Awesome," Zeke said, and then followed T'Challa's lead and changed into his Red Lightning outfit.

T'Challa led the way in. "No flashlights," he said.

Once again, he felt as if the suit helped his vision in the dark. He saw the dents and cracks in the walls, felt the air around him stir. He didn't even feel the small wet puddles he stepped through.

They walked single file—Zeke's hand on T'Challa's shoulder, and Sheila's on his. "Can you see down here?" Zeke asked.

"Yes," T'Challa said.

"Good," Sheila replied. "Please don't lead us into a fifty-foot drop into a black hole or anything."

"I won't," T'Challa promised, hoping he wouldn't.

They continued to walk. T'Challa sensed the air in front of him, cool and wet. As far as he could tell, he was in a vast empty space. He didn't sense the impression of any objects or structures. Just *emptiness*.

"Hold on," T'Challa suddenly said.

"What is it?" Sheila asked.

"More steps," T'Challa answered.

"How is that possible?" Sheila asked. "I saw the blueprint. This is the basement of the school."

"We'll see about that," T'Challa said, and led the way down.

It was a short set of stairs, and a weak light pulsed at the bottom.

"I see light," Zeke said.

"Thank God," Sheila added.

T'Challa stepped onto level ground.

"This is a subbasement," Sheila said.

"A basement *under* the basement?" Zeke said in disbelief. "Oh, man."

"Look at this," T'Challa said.

A circular door stood before him, closed shut with a massive iron lock. It reminded T'Challa of the door of a submarine he had once seen in Wakanda.

"Where does that go?" Zeke asked, looking over T'Challa's shoulder.

"I didn't see it on the blueprint," Sheila said.

T'Challa closed his right hand into a fist, and felt the material of the suit tighten around his fingers. "Here goes," he said, and drove his fist through the lock.

The lock fell away with a clang and clattered to the ground.

"Wow!" Zeke said.

T'Challa felt his right hand with his left, amazed. There wasn't the slightest sensation of pain. "The suit absorbs energy," he said.

"Wish I had one of those," Zeke murmured.

T'Challa pulled at the door, which scraped open with a bone-piercing metallic screech.

A tunnel. Darkness loomed within.

There was a moment of silence.

"We have to follow it," Sheila said firmly.

"We do?" Zeke ventured.

"Follow me," said T'Challa, and then he climbed up and in.

The tunnel was narrow and dark. T'Challa sensed dirt and gravel under his knees. The cold and wet sank into his bones.

"What if this tunnel doesn't have an end," Zeke said, "and we just kept crawling and crawling forever?"

"Thanks, Zeke," Sheila said. "Thanks for putting that in my head."

T'Challa concentrated on the task ahead of him. He wanted to get out of the close confines of the tunnel. "If there really is something going on down here," he asked, "how did they get in, with the door being locked?"

"Some other entrance?" Sheila suggested.

T'Challa didn't answer. There was something ahead of him. He could sense it, the dim outline of shapes. "I think we're coming up to the end," he said.

Cool air caressed T'Challa's face. Sure enough, the tunnel led out to an open space. T'Challa had no choice but to roll out and drop to the floor, about two feet down. Zeke and Sheila followed his lead.

"Oww!" moaned Zeke, uncrumpling himself and standing up. "That hurt."

"Being a Super Hero is hard, Zeke," Sheila quipped. "Imagine that."

T'Challa took in the space before him.

"What is this place?" Sheila asked. "I don't think we're under the school anymore."

"Looks like some kind of water system," Zeke said. "Maybe this is an old sewer tunnel. I heard there are all kinds of tunnels under Chicago."

They walked a few feet and T'Challa suddenly stopped. Massive columns supported a structure above his head. "Uh, guys . . ." he said, and then pointed.

Ahead of the trio, two stone arches, built in a Roman

style, butted up against one another. "Where the arches meet," he said.

"In the damp below," Sheila said.

"Which is kind of where we are now," Zeke added, stepping over a murky puddle.

T'Challa felt the coolness all around, a blanket of suffocating damp. He walked forward slowly, but then paused.

He gasped.

Devil's Traps formed a path ahead of him, and then snaked around a dark corner.

CHAPTER
THIRTY-SIX

"Are those—?" Sheila started.

"Yup," Zeke said. "Oh, man. This is creepy."

"We have to follow it," T'Challa said. "We have to." He paused and sniffed the air. "Do you smell that?"

"Smoke," Sheila said.

"Be careful," T'Challa warned them. "Follow me."

Sheila and Zeke followed T'Challa without protest. A narrow path was ahead of them, barely a few feet across, with walls on either side. They followed the mysterious archways until they came to another open area. T'Challa sucked in a breath.

Gemini Jones and the Skulls were gathered around a small fire. Smoke drifted up to become lost in the unseen roof. A voice echoed through the cavernous space, and there was no mistaking it. "What we do here tonight, we do as one," Gemini called out. "Tonight, we summon the Prince of Bones!"

A raucous cheer went up from the Skulls.

T'Challa swallowed hard.

Gemini's voice echoed through the dim light again. "This thing called Magick is a fearsome devil, and is quick to fool those who think themselves as mighty. The doing is in the belief, brother. Believe, and ye shall prosper."

Those were Vincent Dubois's words, T'Challa realized. *The ones from his grimoire.*

T'Challa saw M'Baku there in the crowd. And he was smiling.

"I promised you power," Gemini said. "The Prince of Bones will give us that, and more!" He walked in a circle, T'Challa noticed, just as he'd done at the house in the woods. He was in his element. And he had his audience.

"We have to warn them," T'Challa whispered.

A shaft of light shone down from a crack somewhere above their heads. Gemini and the Skulls looked up as the weak moonlight cast its pale glow. *The night of the gibbous moon,* T'Challa thought.

T'Challa noticed M'Baku again. He looked as if he were

enthralled, under a spell, his eyes wide and full of wonder. Now was T'Challa's chance. He stood up. Zeke and Sheila rose with him. "Gemini," he called.

Gemini Jones turned around. For a moment he just stared, as if he wasn't sure who called him. But then his eyes landed on T'Challa. "Not you again," he said, as if exasperated—and then—"*T'Challa.*"

T'Challa was struck speechless.

Gemini cocked his head and grinned. "Oh, snap! You didn't know your boy M'Baku told me who you are?"

T'Challa winced. This betrayal cut the deepest. *Why did M'Baku do it? Acceptance? Respect?* He didn't understand.

"You know what happens to spies, right, T'Challa?" Gemini taunted. "They get busted." He cracked his knuckles.

T'Challa had to be careful. He didn't have time to become distracted by Gemini's childish bravado.

Gemini cocked his head in curiosity, taking in Zeke's appearance. "What are you wearing, man? That some kind of rat? You Super Rat, man?"

Howls of laughter from Gemini and his friends. M'Baku hung back in the shadows, not speaking, just eyeing T'Challa with a guilty expression.

"I don't know how you found us here," Gemini said. "But in a few minutes, you're going to regret it."

"Gemini," T'Challa said, and his voice did not waver. "You're in danger. All of you."

Gemini scowled. "Not this again." He shook his head back and forth and quirked his lips. "Man, you best run home before you get hurt."

A refrain of *oooh*s went up from his friends, accompanied by a few hand slaps.

T'Challa stared at the ground, jaw clenched. He had to do something, but what?

He raised his head. "Your father," he started.

Gemini's head snapped back. "Didn't I tell you not to talk about my father?"

"The Circle of Nine," T'Challa said.

"Circle of *what*?" Gemini questioned.

He doesn't know, T'Challa thought with dread.

"The words," T'Challa said. "The oath you all had them swear."

The Skulls stopped talking. The sudden quiet felt strange to T'Challa—a foreboding stillness. "'Darkness falls,'" he started, "'and He shall—'"

"I don't know what you're talking about, man," Gemini said, "but you best run home. You're messing with stuff you don't know nothing about."

"You made them all swear on that book," Zeke said.

A murmuring rose from the crowd, but it wasn't in response to Zeke.

"What is that?" Wilhemina Cross whispered.

T'Challa turned, tense and ready.

From the darkness beyond, a shape drew closer. T'Challa leaned forward but couldn't make it out. As it approached, it split apart, like a cell dividing under a microscope.

Men.

Nine men.

And Bartholomew Jones stood at the front of them, dressed in a flowing robe of black.

CHAPTER THIRTY-SEVEN

Mr. Jones and his men stopped in front of Gemini and the Skulls.

T'Challa clenched his fists. He felt the power of his suit, pulsing next to his skin. *What would Father do if he were here?*

But his father wasn't here.

T'Challa had to be the Black Panther now.

He stepped out of the shadows.

Mr. Jones turned. "Young prince," he said. "So you have come to my awakening."

Gemini tilted his head. "He's a fool, Pop. I told him he's got no business here, but he didn't want to listen."

T'Challa took another step forward. "Whatever you're doing, I'm giving you one chance to step away now, before people get hurt."

"Hurt?" Gemini said. "Do you know who you're talking to?"

"My ring," T'Challa demanded. "Where is it?"

Mr. Jones reached within the folds of his cloak. A silver medallion hung around his neck. T'Challa took a step forward.

Slowly, Mr. Jones withdrew his hand and revealed a vial, swirling with silver liquid. "Are you speaking of this?" He held up the vial, and the darkness surrounding them flared.

T'Challa shuddered. *What did he do with my ring?*

Mr. Jones held the vial high, and the roof of the cavernous space brightened. "Did you know that when Vibranium was first found in Wakanda, it turned several of your people into demon spirits?"

"Pop," Gemini said. "What's going on? Do we use that for the summoning?"

Mr. Jones turned to his son. "Oh, there will be a summoning, but it certainly won't be for a dead schoolboy."

Gemini cocked his head again, as if he didn't understand. *What's he talking about?* T'Challa wondered.

T'Challa had a decision to make. He could try to take down Mr. Jones now, or he could let him speak. He remained wary, ready to leap into action, but Gemini interrupted his plan. "We've got the gate, Pop." He pointed to an arrangement of Devil's Traps forming a triangle. "It started at the school. We placed them all around the entrance, so he can follow it here."

"You have done well, my son," Mr. Jones said. "Tonight, you will be shown the higher mysteries, as I promised you."

Gemini turned to look at his followers. He smiled and bobbed his head up and down. "See what I told you? That's right. Glad you stuck with me now?"

Heads began to nod in agreement, but T'Challa saw that several kids remained quiet, and began to turn and look at each other, wondering what they had gotten themselves into.

"This is where he'll come through," Gemini went on, nervous energy coming off of him in waves, "the Prince of Bones. He'll give us power! More than we could ever want!"

But the Skulls did not cheer and applaud this time. They were watching Gemini's father and the silent men who stood behind him.

"I had them all swear on the book, too," Gemini said, turning back to his father. "Just like you told me to."

"Good, my son," said Mr. Jones.

"We have to do something *now*," Sheila whispered through clenched teeth.

T'Challa felt the material in his suit knitting itself together, almost like a living thing. The spirit of the Panther God, Bast, was stirring inside of him, ready to be unleashed.

Mr. Jones took a few steps forward. "There is something

you all need to know," he said, eyeing the crowd. "You see, to accomplish any great deed, there must be sacrifice."

Gemini nodded—still hopeful, it seemed to T'Challa, that his great moment would be played out for all to see.

"Sometimes sacrifice is hard," Mr. Jones continued, "but the rewards are great. For instance, when you all placed your hands upon the Black Book of Signs and spoke the incantation, you swore your souls away."

T'Challa was struck. *Swore their souls?*

Gemini shook his head in a nervous gesture. "But you said the incantation would open the door to the other side. You said those words would bring back Vincent Dubois. They said it in Old Nubian, just like you showed me."

"Darkness falls," Mr. Jones chanted, "and He shall awaken. Swear to Him, and ye shall be rewarded."

Gemini was now pacing in front of his father. "What does that mean? That's not what you told me it meant. You told me to make them swear on the book. I wouldn't have—"

"But you did, boy," said Mr. Jones with finality. "And now the time has come."

T'Challa was speechless, looking at the two of them, father and son, but so much different from himself and his own father.

Mr. Jones stood over the children like a teacher scolding unruly students. "Your souls will feed the Obayifo," he said. "And your reward will be everlasting life. Through him."

"Obey-*what*?" Gemini said. He was afraid. T'Challa

saw it in the way he stood, as if he had somehow shrunk in on himself.

"Oh-bay-ee-fo," Mr. Jones enunciated. "Also known as Asiman. That oath was one of sacrifice. The Obayifo feeds on souls. The souls of children, to be precise." He angled his head and sniffed the air. "In fact, I think he is here now."

The men behind Mr. Jones began to chant. The sound was familiar. *Old Nubian,* T'Challa realized.

The children began to look around warily. T'Challa saw M'Baku peering left and right. Was he looking for T'Challa to come to his rescue?

I have to strike soon, T'Challa told himself. *Courage cannot fail me now.*

"Long ago," Mr. Jones said, beginning to walk and addressing the crowd, "before I found a higher path, I studied particle physics. I worked for years, until finally, I found it—my life's work." He ran a finger along the silver medallion around his neck, which opened with a click. A small glowing bead of red was cradled within. "It is here, the God Particle, and when merged with the energy from condensed Vibranium, it will open a door to another realm, one where I will rise as a god."

Mr. Jones yanked the medallion from his neck and threw it to the ground.

T'Challa rushed him.

But not before Mr. Jones tipped the vial onto the glowing object at his feet.

CHAPTER
THIRTY-EIGHT

A deafening *BOOM* rang in T'Challa's ears and sent him reeling.

The darkness ahead of him was ripped away and replaced by a gaping chasm, ringed with red and purple fire.

"Zeke!" T'Challa cried. "Sheila!"

But there was no answer.

Gemini and the Skulls were nowhere to be seen. T'Challa picked himself up. The black hole in front of him made a noise, like rumbling thunder. Lightning strikes flared within it, pulsing in colors T'Challa could not describe.

And out of it came Mr. Jones.

But he had changed.

A light was traveling through him, like a pitcher being filled with water, but this light was silvery and metallic.

Mr. Jones shook his head back and forth, as if in pain, but he quickly stood up straight, the strange light within him flickering. His face was . . . shifting . . . moving.

The men picked themselves up from the blast and began to chant again. T'Challa could feel it deep down in his bones. Mr. Jones's head was bowed. But then he raised it.

T'Challa shivered.

Where Mr. Jones once stood was something else. Something . . . *inhuman.*

It opened its mouth. Where its teeth should have been was a forest of tiny black spikes. Its eyes were red, and burned with flame. "He is here!" it roared, arms to the heavens. "The Obayifo is here!"

T'Challa stepped back in horror. *How can I stop that thing? I can't.*

There was a flash of purple smoke and then chaos.

Sheila rushed out of the darkness and flung something high over her head. Another burst of purple smoke plumed in the air. Her smoke bombs, T'Challa realized, as it exploded in front of Mr. Jones. She was trying to create a distraction.

"Red Lightning!" a small voice cried out, as a blur of red zipped past T'Challa.

"Zeke!" T'Challa shouted. "No!"

Mr. Jones swatted Zeke away with one hand, sending him crashing into a wall, limp and broken.

T'Challa sped forward and shimmied up one of the arches, turned his body halfway around, and jumped, crashing down on the creature's back. The Obayifo fell to the ground but quickly pushed itself up, flinging T'Challa off.

T'Challa rolled on the ground and sprang up quickly. He charged again, faster than he thought possible, and swung. He missed the beast's head by an inch and smashed his fist into the wall, creating a spiderweb of cracks. T'Challa didn't have time to marvel at his own strength. He just had to fight.

The creature struck out with a closed fist, catching T'Challa in the jaw. He flew back, dazed. It felt like he'd just been hit with a sledgehammer, though the suit dampened the blow somewhat. If it hadn't, he realized, he'd be dead.

T'Challa leapt up off of his feet again and flipped in a backward somersault, driving his foot up into the creature's chin and landing back on solid ground. But at the last moment, he slipped, and they both went down in a tumble, arms and legs flailing.

The two of them stood quickly and faced each other, breathing hard. "For Wakanda!" T'Challa shouted, and charged again. Right at the last moment, he sprang up, higher than humanly possible, and came crashing down, driving his elbow into the hideous creature's spine. It cried out—a deep, unsettling moan—and flung T'Challa from its back again.

They faced each other once more—the young panther and this thing from who knew where. T'Challa's breath was coming in great gulps. He squeezed his fists and felt the cloth of the suit tighten around his knuckles. Behind him, the hole through which Mr. Jones appeared stood open like a giant yawning mouth, black and fathomless.

Then T'Challa saw the kids.

"Help!"

It was as if a giant vacuum had been turned on, sucking up everything in its path, a black hole leading to nothing. Dirt and mud swirled and slid toward the hole. T'Challa didn't have much time.

The Obayifo drew itself up to its full height. A long arm shot out and grasped T'Challa around the neck. He couldn't breathe. He clawed at his neck, trying to break free. The Obayifo slammed T'Challa against the wall, but the kinetic energy of the Panther suit absorbed it.

"See, young prince," the creature said, just inches from T'Challa's face. "Look what you've gotten yourself into now."

T'Challa gagged. The monster smelled of death.

"I will stop you," T'Challa croaked out.

The creature cocked its head. "Really? How?" Its eyes blazed a terrible red.

"Like this," T'Challa said, and crashed his forehead down into the demon's head.

The beast fell back, and T'Challa immediately thrust out his leg, delivering a forceful kick to its midsection, pushing the monster farther back toward the hole.

"Help!" T'Challa heard. Several children were being pulled along the damp floor by the black hole, a force too strong to resist. They grasped at the ground but found no purchase. *Zeke and Sheila,* T'Challa thought with dread. *I have to stop this thing now!*

From the corner of his eye, a dark figure came running in his direction.

Gemini Jones dove headfirst into the demon's chest, knocking it to the ground. T'Challa quickly joined him, grabbing one arm while Gemini clutched the other. They were close to the hole, crackling with energy and fire.

The thing shook its gruesome head and howled, trying to break free, but both boys held it tight. T'Challa felt a pull as the hole tried to swallow him up. Gemini was also being pulled along, as if by an invisible magnet. T'Challa stretched out his other arm against Gemini's chest, holding him back while trying to grapple with the boy's transformed father at the same time.

T'Challa planted his feet, trying with all his might to gain a foothold, as if he were playing tug-of-war back home in Wakanda with M'Baku.

The creature that was once Gemini's father pushed back, using all of its strength to push itself away. But both boys dragged it closer to the swirling empty mass. White lights winked from within its inky depths.

T'Challa looked at Gemini. Gemini looked at T'Challa. And then they pushed the thing in.

CHAPTER
THIRTY-NINE

The black hole winked out, as if it had never existed.

T'Challa thought he saw little orbs of red and green light floating in the air, but he wasn't sure. He was dazed, his head spinning with what had just happened.

The air around them stirred, warmer than it had been just minutes before. It was as if a door had been closed, shutting out the cold air from another room.

There was no scream. No howl of pain. Just silence.

The men, the Circle of Nine, were nowhere to be seen. The only sounds were the soft sniffles and cries from children. Zeke and Sheila crept from behind the arches.

"Is it done?" Zeke asked. "Did we stop him?"

"We did," T'Challa said. "Are you hurt?"

"My arm feels like it's banged up," Zeke said, "and my head hurts."

"It was brave what you did," T'Challa said. "Both of you."

"One for all and all for one," Zeke said.

They were interrupted by the sound of moaning and startled voices.

"Help them," T'Challa said to Gemini.

And without missing a beat, Gemini jogged over to help his friends. For a gang that was supposed to be so tough, T'Challa noticed, not one of them chided the others for crying. They had seen something terrible. Something not of this world.

"I'm sorry," T'Challa heard Gemini confess a short distance away. "I . . . I didn't know. I didn't know my father used me to do this. I wouldn't've— I couldn't . . ." He trailed off, and raised his hand to his eyes. He shook his head, and then his voice broke. "I'm sorry," he said again.

Small pools of lights from several cell phones began to glow. A jumble of mingled voices reached T'Challa's ears:

Someone call 9-1-1. . . .

I need to call my parents. . . .

Who was that in the black costume? The one that was fighting it?

T'Challa found his backpack and darted away unseen, behind one of the many dark spots in the underground tunnel. He slipped his clothes on over the Panther suit and found Zeke and Sheila. "We have to get out of here," he told them.

"What was it?" Zeke asked, looking around warily, as if another monstrous creature could appear out of the darkness. "How did—?"

"Gemini's father," Sheila said, her voice faraway and quiet. "He was . . . He changed into . . ."

"He's gone now," T'Challa said. "Whatever it was, it can't hurt anyone again."

He turned and searched the throng of kids for M'Baku, but he was nowhere in sight.

CHAPTER
FORTY

Back outside, the air was cold and damp, but T'Challa was still burning with adrenaline. They walked through the empty parking lot of the school, silent. The moon was dim above them.

"I can't believe it," Zeke said.

"*No one's* ever going to believe it," Sheila added.

"Except for everyone that was there tonight," T'Challa said. *They saw me. They all saw who I really am.*

When T'Challa slept that night, his dreams were full of black fire and smoke. He awoke several times gasping for breath, believing that the Obayifo, the monstrous creature from the depths of the underworld, was there in his room, searching for him. But when his eyes adjusted to the dark, the only thing he saw was moonlight peeking in through his window.

M'Baku came back to the embassy the next day, backpack in tow and with a look of guilt on his face he couldn't hide. He sat on the edge of the bed and put his head in his hands. It took a long time for him to speak, but finally, it all came out.

"It all started with Gemini," he said. "He told me that his father traveled in Africa before and wanted to talk to me."

T'Challa listened but remained rigid, barely making eye contact, only studying the blank walls in the room.

"He was . . . strange," M'Baku continued. "I didn't want to tell him anything. It just sort of happened."

It seemed to T'Challa that he was telling the truth, but he still couldn't forgive him. Not yet, at least.

"He kept pressing me about where we were from, and somehow I—I let it slip. I'm sorry, my friend. Really."

T'Challa was still fuming. "What about my ring?" he hissed. He stood up, and moved closer to M'Baku. "That was your own idea, right? You wanted to impress Gemini and his father! How could you, M'Baku?"

M'Baku lowered his head.

Rage filled T'Challa's heart. He clenched his fists. "This

will come back to haunt you one day," he said. "This . . . betrayal."

M'Baku stood up. The two boys faced each other, breathing hard. But before it came to blows, M'Baku picked up his pack from the floor. "I guess I won't be staying here any longer," he said, and headed for the door.

"M'Baku," T'Challa said wearily. "Just stop. You have to stay here. My father—"

M'Baku froze, and then turned around.

"Wakanda was attacked," T'Challa told him. "Didn't you hear from your father?"

M'Baku slipped his bag from his shoulder. "No."

"Don't worry," T'Challa said. "Everyone's safe. But my father—your *king*—ordered us to stay here until everything is under control. You can't just go running off to who knows where."

M'Baku took a few steps and slumped into a chair. He let out a labored sigh and ran his hand through his hair. "You're not going to tell my father, are you?"

T'Challa didn't answer.

"If he finds out what I've done, he'll never forgive me, T'Challa. He'll banish me . . . make me leave the kingdom."

T'Challa met his friend's eyes. "I don't know," he finally said. "I really don't know what I'm going to do."

And the boys didn't speak again for the rest of the night.

"'Obayifo,'" Zeke read from his cell phone, "'also known as Asiman, is an African vampire demon. It has an appetite for ripe fruit and'"—he swallowed—"'*children*.'"

T'Challa, Sheila, and Zeke sat outside on the football bleachers. The Monday after "the Event," as Zeke called it, several students called in sick. But T'Challa was okay, and so were his friends. And that was all he cared about at the moment.

Zeke fiddled with the clip that held his sling in place. "It's kind of cool, actually," he said. "Having a sprained arm. It gets me out of gym class."

There was a moment of silence.

"How did he do it?" Sheila asked. "Mr. Jones? How did he turn into it?"

T'Challa still wasn't sure, but he had a theory. "I think that the energy stored in that God Particle combined with condensed Vibranium ripped a hole in our dimension."

"But how did he *turn* into it?" Zeke asked. "The Vibranium didn't do it, did it?"

"No," T'Challa said. "Vibranium is an alien metal. It's not magic. I think Mr. Jones and this Circle of Nine mixed magic and science *together*. Remember the chanting? I think that's what really turned Mr. Jones into that creature."

T'Challa remembered the words Mr. Jones had spoken: *Did you know that when Vibranium was first found in Wakanda, it turned several of your people into demon spirits?*

T'Challa shuddered. He recalled the legends of Wakanda, which spoke of his ancestors transformed by their first experience with Vibranium. It was Bashenga, the first Black Panther, who prayed to the Panther God for strength in defeating them.

T'Challa looked out past the football field. Silent crows sat on the fence like sentries. His ring was gone, lost in a swirling mass of energy.

He wondered, not for the first time, what he would say to his father.

CHAPTER
FORTY-ONE

Gemini Jones wasn't seen in school again. The newspapers reported that his father died in a mysterious accident in an abandoned water tunnel.

But T'Challa knew the truth, and so did a dozen other kids. They had all watched as the creature called the Obayifo took possession of Mr. Jones's body.

With Gemini Jones gone, the Skulls no longer had a leader. It seemed to T'Challa that they would have been better off staying close to each other, finding a bond in their unbelievable shared experience. Instead, they drifted apart.

But some of them must have talked about what had happened that night, in the damp below, where the arches meet.

There were rumors flying around school about a boy with a sleek black outfit who moved with unnatural speed and single-handedly defeated the creature. But the stories were vague, as if no one could exactly pin down what had happened. *It was dark,* some said. *It all happened so fast,* said others.

T'Challa wanted more than anything to put that awful night behind him, so he began to study harder than ever before. He buried himself in schoolwork, taking on extra courses and after-school activities. He even went back to his chess matches with Zeke.

As for M'Baku, T'Challa had no idea where he was. He had stayed that first night after the battle and then vanished.

One week to the day from when T'Challa and his friends ventured into the school's basement, there was a knock at his embassy room door. He paused, curious.

Knock. Knock. Knock.

There it was again.

Perhaps it was Zeke or Sheila.

T'Challa walked to the door and looked through the little peephole. He drew in a breath.

It was the man with the eyepatch.

The one who had been spying on him since he arrived.

T'Challa's heart leapt into his throat. He looked around the room for an escape route.

"Open the door, T'Challa!"

T'Challa flinched. *He knows my real name!*

The voice was strong and deep, and seemed to shake the very door itself. T'Challa stepped back. He scanned the room for a weapon, anything that could help him. Maybe this man was an associate of Mr. Jones. He could be another member of the Circle of Nine!

The doorknob rattled from the other side. T'Challa heard a few clicks, as if it were being picked.

And then it opened.

CHAPTER
FORTY-TWO

T'Challa raised a fist to strike, but the man quickly reached out and smothered it with his own, clad in a black glove. T'Challa crumpled under the man's strength.

"T'Challa," he said. "I'm not here to hurt you. Your father sent me."

The man released his grip, and T'Challa took a few steps back into the room. He still didn't trust him, and eyed the man warily. He was dressed all in black, with a leather jacket that looked like it held a dozen mysteries. And then there was the eyepatch, held in place by a band that circled his bald head. The man closed the door behind him.

T'Challa didn't have many options. Clearly, the man

was much stronger than he was, judging by his grip. If T'Challa had the suit, perhaps it could be an even match. But he didn't. It was locked in the safe just a few feet away.

"Mind if I sit?" the man asked, solving T'Challa's predicament on what to say. T'Challa only nodded.

The man sat down and looked around the room. "I heard you had some trouble a while back," he started. "Mr. Jones, I believe. Nasty piece of work."

"You said you knew my father," T'Challa said, ignoring him, even though he wondered how this man knew about Bartholomew Jones. "How can I trust you?"

The man crossed his long legs and let out an exhausted breath, as if he had explained this several times before. "Your father is T'Chaka, the ruling Black Panther and King of Wakanda. He sent you and your buddy M'Baku here for schooling. South Side Middle School. You were both doing pretty well for yourselves—at least *you* were—until your friend M'Baku fell in with the Skulls. And then that whole business with Bartholomew Jones." He paused and shook his head. "I have to say, you did pretty well. I'd say your first mission was a success."

T'Challa's head spun. "How . . . what . . . how do you know all this?"

"My organization has some toys that even Wakanda would envy." He raised a long finger to the ceiling. "Satellites. And some silent surveillance drones. We saw everything.

Just consider it a form of backup. I don't think your father would be too happy if things got out of hand."

"Out of hand!" T'Challa finally raised his voice. "People almost died out there! Mr. Jones *did* die out there! And you saw it all and did nothing? Who are you really? Tell me."

"Sorry for all the intrigue," the man said. "Your father always did say I go on too long."

He reached in one of his many pockets. T'Challa tensed, but the man slowly drew out a slim black metal case and flipped it open. T'Challa leaned forward to read it.

NICK FURY
Director

S.H.I.E.L.D.

T'Challa straightened back up. He'd heard of this man and the organization. "You're . . . *that* Nick Fury? My father's friend?"

Nick Fury almost smiled. "Well, your father's friendship doesn't come easy—but yes—I'd say I'm *that* Nick Fury.

Your father put the word out to S.H.I.E.L.D. that you were coming to the States. He asked me to keep an eye on you but to remain at a distance. So that's what I did."

T'Challa sat down on the bed. He shook his head. He should have known his father would have someone looking out for him. He'd thought that exact same thing a while back when he first saw this man, Nick Fury.

"So what now?" T'Challa asked.

Nick Fury leaned forward. "Now we're going on a little trip."

T'Challa swallowed.

"Trip? So I'm leaving the embassy? What about M'Baku?"

Nick Fury grinned. "Oh," he said. "I already took care of him."

CHAPTER
FORTY-THREE

By "took care of him," what Nick Fury meant was "threw him into an unmarked black SUV and took him to an unknown destination," the same place T'Challa was now headed.

"Your buddy M'Baku was a little harder to convince," he told T'Challa. "So I had to be a bit more . . . persuasive. I found him at Wilhelmina Cross's house. Told her parents I was his guardian. Took a little convincing, though."

Serves him right, T'Challa thought, still upset at what his friend had done. He'd never been under a spell. It was betrayal, plain and simple.

"What about my friends?" he asked. "Zeke and Sheila. Will I get to see them again?"

"I believe that can be arranged," Nick Fury answered.

The trip was long, and the SUV—if that's what one would call it, as it was longer than most—was tinted with black windows all around. T'Challa couldn't even pass the time looking out at the city streets. But he did have a few comforts, including every type of snack known to man, dozens of movies, and any kind of beverage he could wish for—from lemonade to hot chocolate. Plus there were video games, which he played on the built-in monitors, but he really wasn't in the mood for them. Several small screens embedded in the black leather seats showed hot spots and unusual activity in danger zones across the world. T'Challa saw one that read: WAKANDA CALM AFTER RECENT SKIRMISH. He breathed a sigh of relief.

After another hour of traveling, the car finally stopped. Nick Fury hadn't spoken much at all during the trip. T'Challa did have questions, but to tell the truth, he was hesitant to ask him anything. He wasn't afraid of him. He was just wary.

Once outside the car, T'Challa peered around. It was dark, and the city skyline was nowhere in sight. The only sign of life was an enormous aircraft hangar with a few people busily running back and forth, working on something that looked like a giant engine.

"Follow me," Nick Fury said.

T'Challa followed him as he headed into the aircraft hangar. There were nods from the workers and a few grim smiles, but no one spoke. Whatever happened in this place seemed deadly serious.

They stopped at an enormous steel door. Nick Fury pressed a button embedded into the wall and put his eye up against it. There was a click, and the door opened. "After you," Nick Fury offered.

The elevator seemed to take forever going down. It was quiet, and not even the hiss of machinery could be heard. Finally, after what seemed like forever, it softly touched down and the door whisked open.

Rows upon rows of computers lined every wall. Men and women wearing headsets sat at terminals, speaking in a dozen different languages.

"Welcome to S.H.I.E.L.D.," Nick Fury announced.

T'Challa took it all in with wide eyes.

"Take a good look around," Nick Fury said. "Tomorrow morning, I'm taking you back to Wakanda."

CHAPTER FORTY-FOUR

T'Challa looked out from the plane's window, just as he had when he was nearing Chicago. It seemed so long ago now. The gleaming spires of Wakanda's Golden City came into view, surrounded by lush green forests and sparkling lakes and rivers. T'Challa heard the click of a speaker embedded in the seat.

"We'll be touching down in just a few minutes," Nick Fury announced from the cockpit.

T'Challa glanced back at M'Baku, dozing in a seat across the aisle. He had taken the seat farthest away from T'Challa when they boarded the plane. There were several times when T'Challa wanted to tell him to forget that any of this had ever happened—the Skulls, his ring, Gemini's father. But he couldn't. Not now. Not yet.

The previous day, Nick Fury had given T'Challa the "grand tour," as he called it. Every room seemed to hold a mystery—from nanorobotics to artificial intelligence. M'Baku slunk behind him, seemingly uninterested in all the wizardry on display. A few weeks ago he would have been over the moon, but now he seemed like a shadow of his former self.

T'Challa let out a long breath. Butterflies fluttered in his stomach. Not from the plane—but from the prospect of seeing his father again.

T'Challa noticed the effects of war immediately. Several buildings were badly damaged—shattered windows and scorched black spots marred the city's most important structures, including the Vibranium Mound. The pavilions that were set up for his departure were long gone, and now the area was full of military weapons and battalions of troops, still on alert.

M'Baku had been whisked away by one of his father's military aides upon landing. He had shared one last glance at T'Challa before he disappeared. *We'll speak again,* T'Challa thought. *One day.*

When they landed, Nick Fury immediately went to see T'Challa's father, and T'Challa used the time to wash up and rest for a few minutes in his room.

A knock on the door startled him from sleep.

"Come in," he called.

The door opened without the slightest sound, and Hunter walked into the room.

In the short amount of time that T'Challa had been away, it seemed as if his older stepbrother had gained three inches' height. He wore a black uniform with no markings but for a panther's proud face on the sleeve of the upper right shoulder. *Must be the Hatut Zeraze,* T'Challa thought, the secret police force. A beret was cocked at an angle on his head, and T'Challa was reminded of Nick Fury.

"Brother," Hunter said, closing the door behind him. "How are you faring?"

T'Challa decided to try to get things off to a good start. "I'm good, and glad to be back."

Hunter came farther into T'Challa's room. He picked up a small wooden panther from an end table and turned it in his hand. "Father says you got into your own little adventure over there, while we were under attack here."

T'Challa swallowed. *He already knows?* "It was unexpected," he said, "but something that had to be taken care of."

"But you revealed yourself, didn't you? People know who you are?"

T'Challa didn't answer.

Hunter set the small sculpture down. He looked around the room as if he had never seen it before, although he had, many, many times. "It's a burden to be a leader," he said lazily. "Some people just aren't cut out for it."

T'Challa refused to take the bait.

"Maybe you can come by the training camp tomorrow," Hunter suggested. "You'll see some of my new recruits. Not all of them will make it into the Hatut Zeraze, but they'll try."

T'Challa was reminded of Mr. Blevins and his first day of gym class.

Hunter let out a long breath. "I'll be seeing you, brother. It's great to have you home in one piece."

T'Challa swallowed his pride. He remembered how, in the midst of the trouble here in Wakanda, he had asked his father if Hunter was hurt. He didn't want that to happen, no matter how much they fought. Maybe they could start anew—try to forget their troubled history. He let out a breath. "You, too," he said. "It's good to be home."

T'Challa hesitated with each step he took, just like he had when the Dora Milaje called him and M'Baku from the forest. Now they stood guard, silent and unmoving. They stepped aside to let him pass, spear points lowered to the ground.

T'Challa released a breath and entered the Royal Palace. The air here was immediately cooler. Torches in the wall every few feet illuminated the way. His father rose when he saw him. "T'Challa," he called. "Welcome home, son. Come, let's walk."

T'Challa was glad to leave the palace. It was so formal, and he often felt like a child when he stood before the king's throne.

"Nick Fury told me everything," the king said, leading T'Challa away from the city center and along a forest path. "Why didn't you tell me of this threat? This man . . . Bartholomew Jones and these . . . Skulls?"

T'Challa focused on the forest floor beneath his feet. "I didn't want to . . . trouble you. You said I needed to learn how to lead one day. That is what I tried to do."

"Trying to save M'Baku was a good thing, T'Challa. But sometimes people choose the wrong road, and there is nothing we can do to steer them away."

They walked a few moments in silence. T'Challa breathed in the fresh Wakandan air. He didn't realize how much he had missed it. "M'Baku," T'Challa couldn't help but ask. "What will happen to him?"

"That is for his father to decide."

"But you're the king. You can choose any punishment you see fit."

The king stopped on the path. "But I am not his father. He will talk to M'Baku first, and then I may pass judgment, if need be."

T'Challa thought back to all that M'Baku had done, but still, he felt for him. They were friends once, but he sought power and respect elsewhere. Now their friendship was shattered.

A mynah bird made its distinct call, and somewhere far away an answer was returned. "Nick Fury," T'Challa said. "You had him looking out for me the whole time. I thought you trusted me."

"I do trust you, T'Challa, but you were a prince in a strange land. I would have been foolish not to have someone looking out for you."

He did have a point. T'Challa would probably have done the same thing if the tables were turned.

After a moment, his father spoke again. "These friends you found, Ezekiel and Sheila. They know who you are now."

T'Challa felt ashamed, as if he had let his father down. "I had to be honest with them. They helped me, and followed me where I led them. I couldn't deceive them any longer."

"There are times when one has to be true to one's own sense of honor, T'Challa. I think you made the right decision."

T'Challa smiled.

They continued to walk, and as T'Challa followed his father along the forest path, he felt a sense of peace. His thoughts were interrupted by the chiming of his watch. He looked down at it. *Who could that be?*

He pressed the watch face.

To his surprise, the beaming faces of Zeke and Sheila were projected in front of him.

"T'Challa!" they both shouted.

T'Challa looked at his father. "How did they—?"

The Black Panther smiled, a rare treat for anyone fortunate enough to experience it. "I had Nick Fury make a special delivery," he said. "Now you can keep in touch."

T'Challa looked back to the hologram of his two friends.

"This is so cool!" Zeke almost squealed.

"Calm down," Sheila scolded him.

"You calm down," Zeke shot back.

T'Challa watched as the two of them jested with each other.

"When are you coming back?" Zeke asked. "We could use some heroes on the South Side."

T'Challa smiled and looked to his father, who raised an eyebrow and leaned his head into the frame. "You never know," he said.

Zeke swallowed. His eyes widened. "Is that . . . Oh my God. It's the Black Panther!"

"The *real* Black Panther," T'Challa added.

"For now," said the king.

"It's good to see you guys," T'Challa said. "Sorry to leave without saying good-bye."

"It's okay," Sheila said. "We understand. But I've got one question."

"What?" T'Challa asked.

Sheila smiled. "When's the next mission?"

ACKNOWLEDGMENTS

Thanks to everyone at Marvel Press and Disney Book Group for the opportunity to work on this great project. A special nod goes out to Hannah Allaman, a fantastic editor with a keen eye and a creative soul. Your insights really helped me see the story, and for that I am grateful. I'd also like to thank Emily Meehan and Tomas Palacios for their support and encouragement. I would be remiss without mentioning my friend, photographer Erik Kvalsvik, whose photograph graces the back flap on this book and others. He always casts me in the best light. To my family and friends, thanks for your enthusiastic support. And for Julia, this time, more than ever.